BOUNDLESS MAGIC

REDFERNE WITCHES BOOK 2

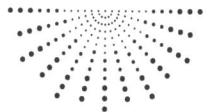

K M JACKWAYS

OLD SOULS PRESS

BOUNDLESS MAGIC

By K M Jackways

Copyright © K M Jackways 2021

This book is copyright. Apart from any fair dealing for the purpose of private study, research, criticism or review, as permitted under the Copyright Act 1994, no part may be reproduced by any process without the permission of the publisher.

A catalogue record for this book is available from the National Library of New Zealand.

ISBN [978-0-473-56340-0] (ebook)

[978-0-473-56339-4] (paperback)

Cover by Jacqueline Sweet

This is a work of fiction. Names, characters, businesses, events and incidents are the products of the author's imagination. Any resemblance to actual persons, living or dead, is purely coincidental.

※ Created with Vellum

CHAPTER ONE

*H*azel pulled her coat closer around her. It was a chilly Dunedin evening and the autumn wind teased at her hair. She watched the traffic navigating the Octagon, listening to people's thoughts as they left work and rushed home. A man unlocking his car was stressed that he had to go straight home and clean the guttering, and the woman walking towards her radiated the guilty feeling of staying too many hours at the office.

On that note, she shrugged uncomfortably, remembering that her mum had rang earlier, and checked her phone. Sure enough, a notification of a voicemail was waiting.

Who leaves voicemail messages these days? she thought, ringing through to her inbox. She leaned against the cool stone of the Town Hall to escape the wind.

"Hi Hazel, it's only me, your mother. I was just calling to ask you if everything was ok. Your aunt—"

The hairs on the back of her hand lifted, and she thought it was her sixth sense picking something up. But when she looked down, it was only a little brown house spider. She

1

shook her hand, taking care not to squash it, and it dropped off.

A mint green Zephyr rumbled up to the kerb and Hazel stood up, slipping her phone into her pocket. Joel reached across to get the latch and the door bounced on its hinges as it swung open in the wind.

He grinned at her, and Hazel could feel a matching smile spreading across her face.

"Hi," she said, dropping into the leather seat. "Thanks for picking me up again."

Joel had offered to drop her off at work and pick her up most days this week. Hazel could easily have biked but he insisted. The days were getting colder but not yet the frosty chill of Southern winters. As usual, no matter the weather, he was wearing a t-shirt. Hazel was grateful that he was, noticing the fine muscle lines beneath his shirt sleeves.

"It's all good," he said, rolling the steering wheel around. "How was your day at work?"

She breathed out. "It was good," she said. Christo, her boss, had been leaving her alone for the most part, and Sia had given her the lead on promotion for a big city event. "Veni, vidi, and I came up with some blooming good ad copy for the flower festival."

"Nice," he said. "I want to take you home a different way today. If that's alright?" He glanced over at her, raising an eyebrow.

She nodded and felt a warm glow right around her ribcage. It was cute when he wanted to show her things.

At first, she couldn't see anything but the green and orange of changing leaves, but as they moved forward, she saw a half-timbered house with gable windows through an archway of trees. It was covered in wisteria and foxgloves nodded from the garden in purples and pinks.

"Beautiful," she breathed, wondering if a witch lived there. It was the sort of place Hazel would love to own one day.

"I saw it last week when I was out here fixing someone's fence and thought of you. You said you liked foxgloves?" He watched her face.

She nodded. "Most people hate them because they are poisonous. But I think no plant is good or bad. It depends on how you use it. That's what Mum always used to say."

It was funny how bits of her childhood and magic lore floated back to her, now that she was using magic again; a memory of her mother rose up, blonde hair tied up and face damp with steam. She could remember the clean smell of daphne, and snippets of songs about plant magic.

Hazel had been practising simple spells in her weekends, but had failed so far to do anything more complex. Telepathy and teleportation came easy to her. A luck charm or healing potion, not so much.

"Digitalis," she remembered, using the Latin name for foxgloves. "It can be used in tiny amounts to increase the contractions of the heart. And also... in love potions."

"You're joking!" Joel said, laughing. Then he turned the car back up the hill toward home, glancing across at her. "You're not joking?"

"No. It's actually true," she said, and chewed her fingernail, wondering if he would ask whether she, Hazel, had used one on him. But Joel was quiet for a moment.

"That's all I wanted to show you," he said, finally. "Oh, but guess what turned up on my doorstep?"

"I'm not sure," she said, fiddling with the fan on her side, so warm air blew onto her face.

"A rental agreement and a direct debit form. I reckon my

cousin must have dropped it off." He shrugged. "It was going to happen sometime."

"Ouch." She grimaced. "You don't seem too worried about paying rent."

"I mean, leaving was what I was most annoyed about," he said. "And I can stay living there. So it's fine, I suppose."

Hazel frowned.

"I see Kirsten was nominated for an environmental award recently," Joel added, grinning like he knew it would get her fired up.

"Ugh," she said. "None of this is fine. Why did all those people help Kirsten out? There was your cousin, Scott, and then Mandy at the bank. And my boss, Christo, is involved somehow too. They can't all be worried about some lizards. Something's rotten and I don't like it."

He shook his head. "Do you think you can let it go for now? You need to relax," Joel said, rubbing her shoulder with one hand. Hazel leaned into it, like Bonnie did when getting an ear rub. She felt some of the stress melt away as his fingers kneaded into the muscle alongside her spine.

As nice as it was, Hazel thought 'letting it go' was the last thing she needed to do. Mandy was Kirsten's sister-in-law, so she would be able to tell her something useful. But Mandy knew Hazel was a witch and she might be able to guard her thoughts. If only she could get close enough to listen in somehow.

And she still had the whole issue of the magical creatures living under their properties, that possibly needed protection.

Joel squeezed her shoulder with one hand. "Are you listening? You might be a…" He hesitated, still unsure of the word in his mouth.

"Witch," Hazel whispered, throwing the bait out between them, waiting to see if he would pounce on it or treat her gently.

"A badass witch," he said. "But you're still a person. And you need to take care of yourself. Oh damn," he added, softly, peering at the dashboard.

"What?"

"It's just that we're almost out of juice." He said it lightly, but she looked over at the needle on the dashboard, which was right on the line. "I can get us home, don't worry. If we can make it up this hill, then we can coast down the rest of the way."

He stepped on the accelerator and the car kept its speed up on the hill. From the corner of her eye, she noticed the spider abseiling down on its silk, hovering just over the back of his neck, its legs wiggling ever so close to the sensitive hairs. So it had stayed attached to her before.

Not now. Joel hated spiders. He didn't need that distraction.

Hazel saw it all play out: the spider landing, his hand reaching behind to wipe away a hair, finding it was a spider and flinging it off to land in his lap. The swearing. The pulling over. The stress. Her pulse raced.

She sent out a little magic and gently grabbed the string, floating the spider down to the ground behind the front seat. He would never know.

"Nearly there," he said. He turned to grin at her, as the car groaned its way over the crest of the hill.

Hazel let out a breath. "We made it," she said, thinking how dramatic that sounded. But things hadn't been easy.

For the past two weeks, they had been trying to organise a date, talking carefully, like Hazel's mother handling foxgloves.

When Joel saw the spirit of her grannie, he had walked out the door, literally without looking back. Hazel was surprised he didn't run.

"I think I might need to stay away from your place for a while," he had said, after sulking for almost a week. "Until I can get my head around it."

"If that's what you need," she'd replied. "We can hang out here." She patted the unpainted back side of the door of Joel's cabin, with hooks for their jackets. "It's tiny but I love it."

"Should we just start everything over?" Joel had asked then. "Go out somewhere like a normal couple."

A normal couple, Hazel thought. She wondered what that looked like. In the past, she had been one half of a witch couple. Then she had been a single non-practising witch. Now, she was a witch dating a very down-to-earth bloke. She felt a little thrill of excitement at the thought.

Joel squeezed her in a hug. "I haven't mucked it up too much?"

"Hmm." She screwed up her face, pretending to consider for a second, then shook her head. "Nah. I think we owe it to ourselves to give it a try."

CHAPTER TWO

Why did you do that? Bonnie lifted her head up and stared at her accusingly as she came in the front door. Her familiar had obviously been watching for her at the window to tell her off when she got home.

"Do what?" She didn't bother asking how Bonnie knew. Their connection was stronger than ever these days. As Hazel's power grew stronger, the familiar connection seemed to link them over a longer distance than ever.

Hazel put her bag on the hall table. The house was chilly and Hazel thought it was about time to start lighting the old potbelly fire in the evenings.

Use your powers. You know about The Threefold. The husky's silver ears were standing up to show how serious she was.

"He wasn't going to make it up the hill if he didn't concentrate. And he absolutely hates spiders," she said. "Anyway, how would that come back to me times three?"

It's the fact that you interfered in those lives. You took away his choice to ignore the spider and keep going up the hill, the dog said, padding along behind her. *He could have sorted it out.*

7

"Yeah, I guess," she said, with a sigh. "Come on, I'll take you out the back."

Hazel opened the screen door and watched as the dog hobbled down the back steps. Her heart squeezed. It had been three weeks since Bonnie's front leg was broken. Bonnie wasn't that old, but she seemed it at the moment. And she had a terrible attitude to go with it.

The biggest insult had been the plastic collar she had to wear - the 'cone of shame'. When it was put on, Hazel patiently explained that it was to stop her licking her leg or worrying at the cast while it healed. Bonnie understood the reasons completely, but that didn't stop her staring up at Hazel resentfully from her basket in the following days.

"It's just there in case you forget," she said, kneeling down and stroking Bonnie's face. "If you wake up in the night and your reflexes take over or something."

Bonnie lifted her head. *Well, how would you like it?* Her nose moved as she sniffed. *You've got a bite on your ankle. I can smell it. Shall I put gloves on you, so you can't accidentally scratch it?*

"Touché," Hazel said, trying not to think about how itchy her ankle was now. She smoothed Bonnie's fur back from her face and dug her fingers in, itching the furry neck where the collar sat.

The other thing had been getting Bonnie to take the painkillers. First, Hazel tried crushing them. She couldn't hide them in the dog food, because their connection meant Bonnie knew what Hazel was doing. Then Hazel tried a method recommended by the vet, sticking them down Bonnie's throat, which was just about as bad as it sounded. This ended with Bonnie stubbornly refusing to open her jaws at all, so Hazel's fingers slipped round her teeth when she tried to administer the medicine.

Finally, she tried ignoring Bonnie until she begged for them.

I'd really like to sleep, Bonnie said. *I saw on the Discovery Channel that we need over 12 hours sleep a day.*

"Then sleep," Hazel said, putting the laundry into the machine, and turning it on. She wished for twelve hours of sleep a night, too. Her nights had been restless since the incident with Kirsten, hearing noises every time she turned over and waking tangled in the sheets in the morning, although Briar had assured her she was safe.

I can't sleep, Bonnie growled. *Every time I put my head down, there is a noise. Sometimes it's a pesky bird outside. Or someone down the street putting their rubbish in their bin. Once, a fly woke me up. It wasn't even in this room. Then once I'm awake, I'm awake, because of this damned leg.*

Hazel made sympathetic noises, but didn't say anything.

Bonnie huffed and looked down at her leg. *It's so itchy. It feels like fleas are jumping around inside it.* She rested her muzzle on the carpet, blinking long and slow. *I'm just so sleepy. Maybe... Oh, alright, you win. Would you get me one of those pills of yours?*

Hazel grabbed the little container of pills and held one out on her palm under Bonnie's nose.

The next day, a tiny bottle appeared in the letterbox. Holding it up, she saw it was wax-sealed and tied in twine. It had one of Fritha's home-made labels on it, with 'For Bonnie' inscribed in round letters, and turned out to be a potion that helped to quicken the healing. Hazel sent a quick blessing to her cousin, and vowed to stop in and see her soon.

As Bonnie improved, she became more frustrated with not being able to leave the house. She sat at the back door and made a little whining noise, but she strongly denied *that* when Hazel pointed it out. When she could walk again, Bonnie paced the garden.

The way she walked up and down, like a caged wolf, brought Joel to Hazel's mind. Since they had cleared the air, she went over to the tiny house for a cup of tea a few times a week. When he picked her up from work, they sometimes chatted leaning over the car, in the driveway, with the sweet scent of roses around them and the shadow of the cottage stretching long on the ground. But she still felt like they were engaged in a very specific dance, of which she didn't quite know the steps.

Hazel sat on the verandah steps and got her phone out to listen to the message while Bonnie padded slowly around the edges of the lawn, stopping to smell a blade of grass now and then.

She shouldn't have used her magic, she knew that. Any energy sent out into the world comes back times three. But the spider being in the car was her fault anyway, since she had jumped in with the tiny insect hitchhiker on board, so getting rid of the problem cancelled it out, she thought.

"Hi Hazel, it's only me, your mother. I was just calling to ask you if everything was alright. Your aunt said Moira had used the tarot cards, and your name came up. Call me back. The cards don't lie."

Hazel knew that wasn't how tarot worked, so her aunt must have been asking about Hazel specifically. She slid the phone back into her pocket. She wasn't impressed with the witch grapevine, and she didn't need them calling her future before she lived it.

A faint smell of burning reached her as if one of the farmers nearby was having a controlled burn-off. She looked around the nearby hills for the telltale twist of smoke but the skyline was clear.

"Can you smell that?" she asked Bonnie. It reminded her of yuletide or birthday cakes with her parents, but there was another layer to the smell.

Mm, Bonnie said in a low growl, nose twitching just above

the ground. She followed the scent past the vegetable patch with its spinach going to seed, and along the fence line towards the back corner.

Hazel followed, picking her way through the bark behind the tree, not sure what she was looking for. The leaves on the ground were damp-smelling but there was something else. A sweet, burnt scent hit her in the back of the nose.

She looked down. Something pink was sticking up from the leaves and for a moment she thought it was a lipstick. Picking it up, she could see it was the stub of a thick candle burnt down to the length of a match.

Here, Bonnie said, and sat firmly next to the tree. Hazel reached down to the trunk about knee height and brought her fingers away smudged in soot.

There didn't appear to be any signs of fire smouldering in the leaves nearby, so she didn't think it was kids playing at arson.

That's the sort of candle used in magical rituals, Bonnie said, and Hazel wondered, not for the first time, what her familiar had seen before they met.

The wind rattled the branches against the fence, and Hazel shivered and reminded herself to check the wards. Something had happened here. And it wasn't a birthday party, she was sure of that.

CHAPTER THREE

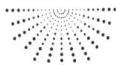

*I*t had rained overnight, and Hazel inhaled the earthy scent as she opened the front door of her cottage. She stood on the verandah, holding her coffee to warm her hands. Silver beads of water clung to the beams above her and dropped off every now and then with a plop.

It was still pretty dark outside but she could just make out the shapes of cars parked out on the road. A lonely Canada goose honked its way across the sky.

"Don't get a fright," came Joel's voice from the darkness. Something white loomed up to her steps and she took a step backwards, spilling hot coffee on her hand.

"What the heck is that?" she asked, shaking the drops off.

She leant forward to have a look. He was wearing gardening gloves and holding something limp, with damp fur and crusted with dark blood.

"It's a dead rabbit," he said, matter of fact. Hazel reeled back from it. "Found it just near the fence down the bottom of the garden. My dad used to take me out shooting sometimes, near Outram. But this is something different."

"Why did you bring it over here?" she asked.

"I just wanted to check it wasn't something to do with... your lot. It looked as if it had been chucked over the fence."

Hazel raised her eyebrows. "Ah, we don't use blood magic around here." He would have known that, if he had ever tried to talk about it with her.

Saying that made her think of the burning smell in her garden, and she wondered whether they both were part of some sort of dark ritual. "My Grannie might know— "

"I better get rid of Bugs here." Joel held the rabbit carcass out in front of him with a wry smile. But it seemed as if he was trying to get away.

Hazel let her breath out slowly. Was it the m-word or the mention of her grannie that had scared him off this time?

Everything dried out, and the clouds burned off in the afternoon. After work, Hazel biked up the hill to Moon Brew under a blue-grey sky, her back burning. Moon Brew was a trendy coffee shop in Roslyn, and her aunt Briar's first love. She had leased the building eight years ago, and the café had slowly built up its reputation with the locals since then.

Hazel waved at Fritha through the window, as she was taking off her helmet. It would be good to have a witch session, and get her opinion on how it was going with Joel.

"I saved you a table," Fritha said, wiping her hands off on her apron as she came out from behind the counter.

"Thanks. It has to be the hottest day in autumn," Hazel said, trying to get cool air into her top, as she looked around. The place was buzzing. Briar's face was red behind the coffee machine but she gave Hazel a little wave.

"You've been busy today?" she asked.

"Yup." Fritha led her over to a small table in a quiet corner near the window. "Over here. I had to pretend it was booked when a group of tourists came in."

"I heard that," Moira said, sidling past with a tray of tea. She was Briar's partner in life and business and didn't take any nonsense from anyone.

Fritha put up her hands. "She's *family*."

Hazel took a seat, and picked up the newspaper. She skimmed over the main article about a woman selling drugs to teens, and one about a medium quake off the coast. Her eye was drawn to a small column about another sighting of a big cat. The feral cats popped up from time to time, from Canterbury to Central Otago, usually in the backcountry, along with photos from a hunter swearing he had seen the large feline.

"Surely I've earned a little break," Fritha said, sinking into the other seat with a sigh. Her cousin looked effortlessly trendy with her blonde hair in braids, a singlet that Hazel knew would be organic cotton, and oversized wooden beads around her neck.

"Thanks for the salve for Bonnie's leg," Hazel said, over the top of the newspaper. "It worked really well. Sorry that I didn't message you to say thanks. I've been busy—"

"With your hot neighbour? Come on, tell me about it. My life is study and *this place*." She indicated the café with a flick of her wrist.

"It is going pretty well. Joel keeps saying that he wants to work at having a relationship," Hazel said. "He seems really keen. But the fact that Grannie is a…" Here, she mouthed the word, 'ghost'. "That's a really big issue for him. Like, he wants to completely avoid all mention of it. He doesn't even want to come over to my place at all."

"Ooh, he's so broody, isn't he?" Fritha absentmindedly took the water glass and started polishing the rim of it with her shirt. "You wouldn't get that just from looking at him."

"Mm." Hazel liked the thought of broody men as much as

anyone, but reflected that it would be easier if Joel was a little less Mr Darcy and a little more upfront. "Are you all working here today?"

"Yeah, we put out a new Irish coffee called Boss Brew. We may have added an extra ingredient to improve concentration. It's selling really well." Her eyes twinkled.

"That's pretty great marketing, though."

"I thought you'd be proud of me," Fritha said, with a smile. "So I didn't feel too bad turning away the tourists, since we're that busy. They did get some free water though," Fritha said, putting her own water glass down and filling it from the jug. "I think they wanted somewhere to hang out, before their street art tour."

"Oh, that reminds me," Hazel said. "Have you seen the mural down Stafford Street?"

She told Fritha about how she had felt while touching the painting of the Haast Eagle. "At first, I could feel the cool of the bricks, then I sort of fell. It was the weirdest feeling ever. I felt like I was inside the scene. I could see the land as it probably used to be, covered in bush, and huge ferns. The ground beneath me was alive with insects and rodents. I could sense them, but it was almost like I *was* the eagle. I knew what it knew, if that makes sense?"

"Not really." Fritha laughed.

"It's probably because I had been reading that book, *The Aotearoa Menagerie*," Hazel said. "Vivid imagination."

Briar was standing beside them, wiping her hands with a red tea towel and looking at Hazel, with her forehead creased in a frown. She was quiet for a long moment.

"Hazel," she said, finally. "Hazel, Hazel…"

"What?" she asked her aunt. She lifted up the newspaper, and scanned it, looking for any events she should avoid. Parades and expos were all well and good, but not when a telepath accidentally walked into the middle of them. The thoughts and moods of a crowd of people made her feel like she was directing traffic in the centre of a busy intersection, with angry drivers leaning on their horns. It was too much.

"I'm speechless," her aunt said, still staring.

Hazel laughed. "You're clearly not."

But Briar wasn't joking. She clicked her tongue. "I told you to be careful. Remember, a few weeks ago, after the attack? But I never thought…"

"Okay, if you don't tell me right now, I'm going to reach in there and take it," Hazel said, motioning to Briar's forehead. She wasn't really confident that she could read her aunt's mind if she was blocking her, but a small part of her wanted to try.

Briar didn't look worried, keeping that calculating stare on Hazel's face, while she wrestled with something. Her aunt's hair was tied back in a loose bun, and she pushed the little strands of chestnut off her face.

If she was reacting like this to something so minor, Hazel wondered how she could tell her there may have been a summoning in her garden yesterday.

"Fritha, can you go help that customer for me, dear?" She folded the tea towel neatly on the table.

Fritha reluctantly got up, and Briar sat down in her seat, her stare burning into Hazel. She pushed her glasses up and rubbed her eyes.

"I was hoping I could wait another ten years for this…"

"For what?" Hazel asked. "It's nothing. Don't worry about it."

Briar sighed. "You were saying that it felt like you were in the artwork? That is *definitely not nothing*. Something very similar happened to me a long time ago."

Hazel was interested now. So she wasn't the only one who had fallen into a painting. "Was it a piece of art?"

Briar tilted her head, considering. "It was in a book. We

found a box of old things in the attic at the Oamaru house. There was this one particular picture of a kiwi that I couldn't stop looking at in one of Grannie's old notebooks. The picture was just sketched, and I don't know who did it. But my mind filled in all the blanks of the picture; the colours, sounds, smells. It was hyper-real." She went quiet for a minute.

"I stared and stared, until I went dizzy," Briar said, smoothing the tea towel over and over. "It was only after I fainted that my mother asked me 'twenty questions' about it. She asked what I was doing beforehand, and I told her about the picture and how it felt like I was in it. She started crying, she said with happy tears, but I'm not sure. And she told me that it was time to pass something on to me." She swallowed a few times.

Fritha came back and set two steaming hot drinks on the table, topped with cream, marshmallows and chocolate sauce.

"It's just coffee, but with a few extras chucked on top," she said, looking back and forth. She narrowed her eyes at the two of them. "What are you two planning? My birthday isn't until November."

"It's not always about you, sweet," Briar said. She stood up, sending silent thoughts to Hazel. *We'll talk about this again soon.*

CHAPTER FOUR

*I*t was a relatively flat ride across the top of the hills back home, but Hazel was still red-faced and sweating when she wheeled her bike down her street.

She paused by the letterbox and wiped her face with her shirt. Just then, Mrs Dowling from number 18 appeared from her pathway. Joel was with her, his tool belt around his waist.

"Oh, Hazel," Mrs Dowling called. "How are you going, dear?"

She stayed where she was, but they crossed over to her. "Hello," she said.

"This nice young man was just looking at my handrail for my stairs. He's going to fix it up for me. What did you say your name was again? Jack?"

"It's Joel," he said.

"We have met before," Hazel said, looking at him and feeling laughter bubble up inside.

"Yeah, I'll just pop home and get my other screwdriver, Lilian." He jogged around to his place and disappeared behind the bushes.

These two seem like they'd be a good match, Mrs Dowling

thought, *although Hazel seems a bit older than him. Perhaps she'd enjoy being a cougar, as they call it.*

Hazel coughed. "Okay, I better go get changed," she said.

Makes me feel alive having a young man in the house. Too quiet with only the ghosts of the past whispering to me.

"Bye, dear." She held up a hand.

Always so busy, that one. The thought floated to Hazel as she turned away, and she rushed up the steps, before she could hear anything else. She felt sorry for the old woman, who'd lived by herself the whole time Hazel had been at the cottage.

But she also knew what it was like to be surrounded by ghosts. What she hadn't confessed to Fritha today was what Joel had said to her after he found out her secrets.

They had walked for miles along St Kilda beach on a grey day, the tussock-covered dunes rising up on one side and the sea on the other.

"You being a… *you know* made a lot of sense to me," Joel said, because of your confidence and the fact that you seem to have so many secrets. It fit somehow. So I could *accept* that, and I even wanted to learn more about it."

Hazel didn't like his use of the past tense, and stopped to pick up a piece of driftwood, to hide her face.

"But the other thing…" He left the sentence hanging for a beat, and Hazel could almost see her grannie's spirit form through his eyes.

"My grannie, Emily Redferne," she said, firmly, "died over fifty years ago. She is a spirit tied to the attic of my aunt's house. Emily is my grandmother's mother, so she is technically my great-grandma. She is an amazing woman, and quite a practical and down-to-earth person, despite her appearance. She's not going to hurt you."

Joel was quiet, and Hazel looked out across the sea, suddenly uneasy. She turned the driftwood over, running her fingers over the smooth wood, shaped like the ears of a rabbit.

"I hear the words you're saying," he said, finally. "I'm sure she is a wonderful person, ah, ghost. I just can't reconcile that with…"

His eyes unfocused as he stared into the distance, and she sensed grief coming from him in waves. It all made sense to her now.

"Your parents," Hazel said, barely above a whisper.

She waited. Sometimes people needed space, and a sounding board. By talking through it, they often found the issue by themselves.

"Mum died six years ago," he said. "Dad died when I was eleven. There was a fire. And Mum passed away after a long battle with cancer." He had his head down, so Hazel couldn't see his face. "I was an only child, so it was always just them and me. The only way I could keep on going was to tell myself they were somewhere better. Where their pain was gone and they had everything they needed."

After a short silence, Joel spoke, and it was so quiet she had to lean forward to hear. "It's fine. I mean, I'm not sad about it anymore. But it chills me to the bone to think of them... What if they are stuck somewhere like that?"

Hazel smiled, sympathetically. "She *is* bound to the cottage. But Grannie's not unhappy. She can be near her family and get involved in things just the way she likes. Boss us around, in other words," she joked.

Joel took a deep breath. "It really is an issue for me," he shrugged. *I'm just not sure how to get over it.*

Hazel just grabbed onto his hand. She was confident that time would heal anything, even this.

It was the next evening when Hazel met Briar at the Mornington viewpoint. She crossed the large circle of grass and stepped onto the wide driveway. It was one of the best views over Dunedin and the harbour. Workers parked there in their lunchtimes to admire the view and lovers parked there to admire each other.

"I'm sorry to be such a secret squirrel about all this," Briar said, when she sensed Hazel coming up behind the park bench. She turned to face her niece with a grin. "This feels a bit like that time I was planning to sneak out with Johnny Mathews. You could tell something was up, and asked why I was anxious. I had to explain the whole thing so that you didn't out me to Mum! Remember?"

"I forgot about that," Hazel said, smiling. She sat down beside her aunt. "What was I? About ten? I would only have been able to read your mood then."

Briar nodded. "Probably about that age. But you always seemed older," Briar said. "Anyway, the secrecy is a bit weird, I know. We couldn't really chat at the cottage, or at the café. Or my house."

"Okay, but listen to this." Hazel told her aunt about the sweet burning smell, the candle and the dead rabbit. "Do you think it might have been a sacrifice?"

Briar tilted her head. "Could be. But I wouldn't be too quick to assume anything," she said.

Her aunt didn't offer any other explanation and Hazel frowned.

"What did you have to tell me?" she asked. "What happened at the street art didn't feel normal, but I wrote it off as an empath thing."

"Well, there are definitely a few of *those*," Briar said. "I'm going to start at the beginning. You know what my role is in the coven, don't you?"

"Yeah." She didn't say it, but everyone in the coven knew that Briar was the Secret Keeper. Not what it meant, but just that she was. Nobody outside of their family was allowed to know.

"It's extremely important. I'm going to let you in my mind now."

Hazel reached out and latched onto her aunt's thoughts.

The Secret Keeper holds our ancestral knowledge. Everything the witches who came before us learned; spells, remedies, who was hexing whom.

I was initiated almost twenty years ago. I've been looking for someone to teach, and it occurred to me a while ago that you would make the perfect person. The tarot card reading, your reaction to the art—all of that just confirmed it.

Hazel started. "Me? What about your own daughter?" Fritha was learning herbal medicine from Aster, Hazel's mother and the oldest member of their coven. She was also studying a Masters in Nutrition. Along with her powers in potions, that made her a very strong witch.

Briar shook her head. "It's got to be somebody who won't accidentally *spill* anything. Someone strong, but not obvious. Look at me, for Goddess's Sake. I can blend in anywhere, the 40-year-old, overweight woman with greying roots." She pulled at her hair. "The Secret Keeper is someone who isn't a target, who can't be cracked. Ever. It has to be someone who people trust."

"We trust Fri—" Hazel began.

"No," she said. "I mean, *we* do, of course. But I've observed the others for a long time, and people in general don't tend to. I'm not sure why. Shallow, but there it is."

"Hello! My red hair stands out," Hazel said, lifting up a lock of hair. "People turn to look whenever I enter a room. I'm not exactly incognito."

"Maybe, but they tend to trust your face. This is the right course of action, Hazel. I knew it when I heard you talking about the street art." Her aunt seemed no longer to be Bry, who was almost like a sibling. Bry, who had taught her what to do for period cramps and commiserated with her over ice cream when she didn't get into the netball team. Hazel could tell from the set of her jaw that she was now speaking as a senior member of the coven.

Hazel's gaze floated over the flax bushes in front, down to the city, the sparkling harbour and the gorse-covered peninsula beyond. It sounded as if she had to look after a spell book, full of knowledge. That couldn't be so hard, could it? It might even help her learn some new spells.

"What exactly...?" She trailed off, not sure what to ask.

"Not now. I want to initiate you on the next full moon," Briar said, leaning forward. "I can promise you it will be absolutely life-changing. But the most important thing for you to do is keep on living your life as you have been. No more digging around in other people's business."

"That's not fair," she said, stung. "I'm not just being nosy for no reason. I helped find out what was wrong with you when you were attacked. Fritha and I saved you." Hazel knew she sounded like a whiny teenager, but that's how she felt she was being treated.

"And I thank you for that," Briar said, leaning against her lightly. She smelt of coffee. "I do. But now it's time to take a step back. Go to work each day, keep your head down. Don't do any speeches or put your hand up for any promotions. Lay low."

CHAPTER FIVE

*A*fter a restless night where Hazel tormented herself with thoughts of magical books and being stuck in the same job for the rest of her life, she dragged herself out of bed.

Joel drove her to work, and she hardly heard what he was saying. She stared out the window, head resting against the cool glass, watching the houses warp and blend into one as they passed by.

He looked over at her. "Do you still want to go on that date?"

"Oh," she said, jolted from her thoughts. "Yeah, of course!"

"What do you want to do? Movies?"

Hazel fiddled with the seatbelt. That was another problem. "Um… I can't really do that. There would be too many thoughts around me, so that I can't even focus on the film." She wasn't usually a fussy date, but with her new psychic sensitivity, dating was going to have to be different. "It would be a bit of a waste of money."

"Oh, right, sure," he said, quickly. "What about a concert?"

Hazel frowned, watching as a few fat drops of rain plopped

onto the windscreen and streamed down. "That's probably not the best, either. The mixture of lots of people and really loud noise is... overwhelming... "

Joel looked so disappointed, that she laughed.

"We can work this out," she said. "I can do plenty of things, but we'll just have to think about it a little. I'd be happy with an early dinner out, or we could watch an old movie at your place."

He pulled over and kept the car running. "Dinner it is. You name the place and the time."

"I'll let you know. And can I tell you something?" This had been on her mind for a while, stewing beneath the surface, and she blurted it out, before she could stop herself. "I haven't dated someone who wasn't a witch before. It's actually brand new for me being able to tell what you're thinking all the time."

She felt her face grow hot and turned to look outside again. The attraction, the falling into companionship as if they'd known each other for years, the collide and rub of strong, independent personalities.

"That's probably why it all happened so fast," she said. "My ex..." She stopped with one hand on the car door handle and let it hang, not sure whether she should talk about Hadley or not.

He motioned to her to go on.

"The *last person I was with* knew how to block me from reading his mind."

Joel let out a long breath. "Right, ok. Well, I can't do that," he said. "I wish I could."

"Yeah."

He pulled back a bit, and looked down at her lips. His thoughts came to her. *I know we're taking it slow. But I can still kiss you, right?*

She started to say yes, but the soft press of his mouth was already on hers.

"I better… " She jerked her thumb at the building behind her. She gave herself a mental slap in the face. It was something about the way she could sense what he was thinking. When they kissed, she wasn't wondering if he was enjoying it or if he was thinking about what to have for dinner. She had to break it off before she melted. "See you later on."

"Looking forward to it," he said, showing his teeth.

Pull yourself together, she thought, as she walked inside, shrugging off her coat. It was stuffy in the office as always.

"What are you smiling about?" Her friend June looked up from her desk, smiling. Her fifties suited her, Hazel thought, admiring the new purple colour she had in her short hair.

Hazel put on her best work face and sat down. "Oh, nothing."

"A certain nothing who is very good with his hands?" June was looking at her, one eyebrow raised, and Hazel stopped. Sometimes, it seemed as if June was the mind-reader, instead of her.

"He makes gorgeous wooden chests *with his hands*." June shrugged in mock innocence. She held out a box filled with chocolate bars. "Here, have something from the box. It's fundraising for my nephew's school. Two dollars a bar - take a couple."

"I haven't got any coins with me," she said, peeking in at the wrappers.

"It's alright. I know where you live, anyway," June said, pushing her glasses down onto her face, to write Hazel's name on an IOU.

Hazel selected something that looked like it would be filled with gooey caramel and wafer pieces, and slipped it into her bag.

She picked up the stack of papers she'd been working on

with a sigh. With the drizzly, grey weather outside, it felt strange to be working on a garden festival.

"Right. Think," she said to herself. She went back through the design brief, before sending it through to the Content Team. She was creating promotional items for the festival, and she had to send through concepts, keywords and some phrases, as well as who the target audience was.

For that matter, it was strange to be at work at all, when she really wanted to be grilling her aunt about the bombshell she'd dropped. "What if I don't want that responsibility?" she would ask. "What if I'm not ready?"

Hazel supposed she should take out some of the attitude in the email she was sending. But she was frustrated and she had brought the fine art of passive aggression into her work. *Waiting on your early response,* she typed.

The real problem was that her aunt hadn't even asked if she was interested in being the Secret Keeper, or wanted to discuss her reasons. Hazel thought that was a bit unfair. It felt a bit like getting a diagnosis, unexpected and completely life-changing.

Could she refuse it? Just say no? She thought of her parents' disappointed faces, and her aunt with no one to pass her knowledge onto. But it would be a big responsibility, and something she would have to keep hidden from Joel.

"You alright, sweet?" June said, coming past with the box of chocolate bars again.

"I suppose so. How warm is it in here today?" Hazel got up to make herself a coffee. When she pressed the sugar button, nothing but a grinding noise came from the machine. She absentmindedly wiggled her fingers and the sugar slid down the bench.

It just wasn't fair. She would have to be that ever-present office worker, who did exactly what was expected, and nothing more. The worst part was that she couldn't talk to anyone about it, she thought.

It was only two hours later when the email came through from Tasha Adams in Design. *Please find attached a draft poster*, it said.

She eyed it, and thought she could put something similar together in ten minutes. It didn't use the subtitle she'd sent through and the colours didn't quite match the brand. The event logo looked more like a farm than a garden festival.

"Wow," she said, under her breath. She might need to chat face-to-face with Tasha. It was time for a complete overhaul.

Hazel chanted 'calm and serene, calm and serene' to herself, silently, while walking through the maze of offices to find the Design Team. Design was hidden behind the IT team in the far corner of the room.

Of course they are. That makes perfect sense, she thought.

She asked the old man sitting next to an empty desk where Tasha was.

He peered at her over his glasses. "She's at a meeting."

The man was thinking that he only had another eight months to retirement, and Hazel smothered a smile. "Whereabouts please?"

"Think it was in Admin. Do you want me to ring through?"

Hazel shook her head and walked past Admin on the way back to her desk. Tasha was in the meeting room with her staff member Lee, their outlines visible through the frosted glass. As she got closer, she saw Sia, her boss, gesturing and nodding, from the front.

Hazel's pen got very hot all of sudden, and she dropped it on the floor and stood there, shaking her hand. Why had she not been invited to the meeting?

Tasha opened the door. "Ooh!" she said. "Are you alright there?"

"I'm fine," she said, as much a reflex as scratching an itch.

"You sure? I didn't get you with the door?"

"Yes, I was actually— "

"Sorry, I've actually got to go. Another meeting." Tasha stepped to the side, pointing down the hall.

She sidestepped me, Hazel thought. *Unbelievable.* Just like I was coming in for the tackle and she had the rugby ball.

"Hazel," Sia said. "I'd like you to work closely with Tasha on your projects. We need the design to be spot on."

"I'm actually trying to do that now," she said. "She just—"

"Come to think of it, you probably should have been in on that meeting," Sia said, and walked away. Hazel found herself gritting her teeth.

Back at her desk, she called Joel. Tonight, she needed easy conversation where she could be herself.

"Are you hungry? Shall we do that dinner tonight?"

He sounded surprised, but happy. "Yeah, I'd love to. And I'm always hungry, you know that."

"I know a little Japanese place down George Street."

"Mm, sounds good."

"Meet you there at six? It will still be quiet then. I'll book us a table." Hazel was looking forward to their date. She decided she was going to dress up, so she went looking in the op shops at lunchtime for a dress.

"Do you want to have a drink after work?" June asked, when Hazel got back to her desk. "I'm going with Sia and some of the others and we've asked Christo as well."

"He won't come," Hazel scoffed. Her boss, Christo, had

been very quiet since the speech Hazel gave. It was almost as if he'd gone back to not knowing who she was.

She typed out a quick email to Tasha.

Thanks! I think we might need another draft of the garden festival brief. I'm holding a Focus Group next week to listen to what people want. I'd like you to help me run it. We can try different versions of the ad copy out. Then run the most popular one.

She added the details. Perhaps Tasha needed to hear it from the horse's mouth, so to speak.

"I feel sorry for the person on the other end of that email," June called over. "You were jabbing that keyboard like Greg in Planning."

"Yeah, I'm a little frustrated," she admitted, looking around. The office had cleared out, as people went home to their families. "I can't come for a drink today, either. I've got a date."

"Mmhmm," June said over the top of her glasses, eyeing the bag with the dress in it. "Good on you, love."

CHAPTER SIX

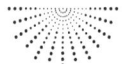

*T*he restaurant was quiet, thank the Goddess, with just two other couples inside. Hazel arrived first, since it was just a short walk from her office. The wind seemed to blow straight down the main street, funneled into a freezing blast. She shut the door on it.

Finding a seat at the back, Hazel took off her jacket, and hung it over her chair. Her dress was a navy blue with ruffles around the neckline. She was probably a little over-dressed for the place, but this *was* something special.

The door jingled, and Joel came in, wearing his normal jeans and checked shirt.

"Evening," he said, rolling up his sleeves.

Hazel felt a warm flush at the sight of him, and his eyes roamed over her.

"You look beautiful."

"Our first date," she said. "That is something to celebrate."

Joel sat down and grabbed the menu. "What are we eating?"

"I think the sukiyaki is always fun," she said. "It's like a soup that you dip—"

"Sounds good! I'm starving."

She laughed. "Let's get some tempura as well. What time do you normally eat?"

"Oh, around six." The server came over, and Joel asked for the food. Hazel looked at the front window, to see if the wind had died down at all, but little bits of rubbish were skidding down the darkened street. She noticed the woman at the table there looking at her, but she quickly looked away when Hazel spotted her. Hazel wondered if she looked ridiculous, like she was trying too hard. She looked down at herself.

"What's the matter?" Joel asked.

"Nothing," she said.

"Like *nothing* nothing? Or actually nothing? Because when I've had girlfriends before, and they say they are fine, or it's nothing…" He shrugged. "It is usually something."

"No, sorry. I would tell you, I promise. First date, right…" Hazel said. She forced herself to look straight ahead, and play the role of a person out on an incredibly normal first date. She owed it to him.

"Joel, is it?" She put on a posh voice. "Okay, well, I'd love to hear about you. What do you do for a job? I don't know why I'm talking like this."

He grinned, playing along. "Delightful to meet you. Joel Anderton. It's always been carpentry for me," he said, then switched to his normal accent. "I started out as a hand, and worked my way up. I somehow ended up working in a windows and doors company, but it was the same thing every day, so I started working for myself. I was a waiter and a kitchen hand for a while before that."

"Really? I'm impressed."

"Don't be," he laughed. "Trying not to burn the soups was about the hardest thing I did. What about you?"

"Well, at one point, I worked as an advertising assistant for a magazine," she said. "Which meant I had to ring up leads and ask them if they wanted to place an ad. Sales, basically. It was pretty bad." She thought for a while. "And I also worked as an assistant to a real estate agent. I had to write up their little blurbs, and ring up after an open home to see if the visitors were interested in putting in an offer. Spoiler alert, they often weren't."

"I knew those people were magicians," he laughed.

"If I was using magic, I would have got more sales," Hazel said, wryly. "And then I got a job promoting events, and it went from there. Where are you from? Have you always lived in Dunedin?"

"Yeah, I imagine you would. My family are actually Scottish, and they came over when I was only six. I don't remember it, but people—"

He broke off as the waiter came over, with a steaming hot pot of soup and a board piled with chopped vegetables and thinly sliced raw meat. He put a burner underneath the pot and lit it with a long lighter. They had their very own fire.

Hazel leaned over to look in the pot. It smelled amazing, and made her mouth water.

"This always feels really primitive, in a way. Sharing food with friends over an open fire," she said.

"Almost like a cauldron," he said, lifting an eyebrow. "Let's get into it."

Hazel grabbed a fork and picked up a piece of carrot, dipping it into the pot. Joel went for the meat. He dropped two pieces in and watched while they changed colour to a light brown in the sizzling soup.

"What were you saying?" she asked, spearing a bit of meat and savouring the delicious flavours. She spared a little glance at the table by the window and saw the woman and man looking over in her direction.

"Oh, yeah, so I was a little lad and I arrived here and went straight into school here. I'd only just had my birthday but it was during the holidays in Scotland. All the other kids had been there for a year already, but I had no idea about school. It didn't help that they couldn't understand my accent. You can't even tell that I'm not a Kiwi, now, eh?"

"Wow. That must have been hard." He nodded. "I mostly hung around with my cousin."

Hazel dipped a bit of cabbage in the soup and offered it to Joel. "Do you mean Scott?"

"Yeah." He shook his head at her offer of food. "Nope. I hate the stuff." *It tastes like someone took some lettuce, threw it in a compost heap and left it to rot for a few weeks...*

"Okay, I did not know that about you," she said, covering her mouth and trying not to laugh. Some people had such strong feelings about vegetables.

Hazel was expected to eat a wide range of naturally available foods as a kid, from walnuts and sorrel root to the yellow gorse flowers. She'd tried some strange mixtures, which her mother said were good for her health. It was *different* having a green witch for a mother.

"I've always lived here in Dunedin," Joel said. "My parents bought that piece of land, and they always said they wanted to farm it. But after the fire, they decided to pull the house down. The insurance was nowhere near enough to build a house back to the required standard on the hill, with foundations and the like. So mum rented another house."

"And you were left with the land." Somehow, hearing that made it even sadder for Hazel that the land had been sold.

"Yeah. Until Whatsherface bought it." There was a pause, and he drummed his fingers on the table. "What do you think is going on with them?" Joel asked, his voice low. He indicated the two men next to the bar, one blond, one almost bald, who looked as if they were having an argument. "I reckon they are fighting over who gets the remote control," he laughed.

"They— " He was just making small talk, and he had

forgotten that she knew exactly what was passing unsaid between the couple. "They want different things."

"Huh," Joel said, looking at her with an inscrutable expression. "Yeah. I guess you do know exactly what they want. He stood up. "I'm just going to find the bathroom."

Hazel glanced over at the window, to see the man alone at the table by the window. He was looking at his phone. She looked back in front and the woman was just sitting down in Joel's chair. Hazel froze.

"Excuse me," the woman said. She had long hair braided into thin plaits and a nose-ring. "I don't normally do this but... I noticed from over there, that something was a bit different about you."

She seemed harmless enough, but Hazel was on edge.

"Because of what I'm wearing?"

"What? No," the woman said, clearly taken aback. "You're going to think I'm a bit odd," she said, looking down at her hands.

"Go on," Hazel said.

"I like to paint," she said. "Ever since I was a kid, I've seen colours in things that other people didn't. Voices, songs. It's really beautiful, actually. It took me ages to realize other people couldn't see them. But—and this is the part that I don't tell anyone—I also see the energy around people."

"That's a gift," said Hazel, smiling. She was relieved, but wondered why the woman had felt the need to tell her. "You are really lucky to have that."

The woman leant forward, and Hazel noticed her fingernails, chipped and with the remnants of a green polish on them. "Your aura is a deep indigo, very vivid, which means you are really intuitive. I haven't seen one like that in quite a while. I can tell you must be a sensitive person."

"Well, yeah, you could say that," Hazel said.

"But when you're around other people, like when the

waiter came over, your energy changed colours... to red, orange, grey. Same thing when you saw me arrive at your table." She fiddled with the serviette.

Hazel stiffened. The reason her energy changed when she was around others, was because she was trying not to hear every thought. This must have been what her aunt was talking about, when she told her that her psychic powers stood out like a beacon. *People will notice*, she had said.

"You don't have to tell me anything," the woman said quickly.

"I just don't like being around too many other people. Bit of an introvert." She tried to laugh.

"I just wanted to tell you what I saw. I do aura cleansing as a bit on the side. Ellie's Energies. Let me know if I can help you in any way." She stood up, and Joel sat back down.

"What was that all about?" he asked, looking after the woman.

"Oh, nothing."

"Nothing nothing?"

"No," she said, trying to make herself believe it. "Actually nothing."

Hazel grabbed his hand, and they continued their meal, but she felt vaguely on edge.

CHAPTER SEVEN

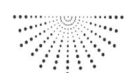

When the car turned down their street, Hazel was surprised to see Briar waiting outside under the streetlight. She wondered why her aunt hadn't let herself inside. It was her house, after all.

"I'll see you tomorrow," she said quickly to Joel, and pecked him on his stubbly cheek. She opened the door on the freezing night.

"Hi, darling," Briar said, when she saw Hazel step out of the car. "I didn't want to scare you. But… oh, wow, have you been somewhere fancy?"

"Not really, it was just a… thing." Hazel pulled her jacket around her. She wasn't sure why but she wasn't ready to officially declare Joel to the family as her boyfriend. Fritha had met him, but the thought of telling the older witches made her feel cold.

Briar was staring at the cottage with her hands on her hips and lips pursed.

"Have you been putting your own protection charms on the property, Hazel?"

"No, I haven't," she said, surprised. "Why?"

Her aunt ran her hand over the bushes, caressing the leaves of the petunia bush. "The ones here seem to be weakening," she said. "They don't have holes in them, but they are sort of, I'm not sure, *thin*. It's like when a balloon is stretched too tight."

Hazel frowned. "Should I be worried?" She thought of the rabbit flung carelessly over the fence, the candle and the burnt patches. Where light flared, shadow also went. And she had the sense that *something had manifested* in her garden.

Her aunt shook her head. "No, I don't think so. But maybe I'll just give them a wee reinforcement while I'm here."

"Okay," Hazel said, and thought of something that always made her feel safe. "Do you want tea?"

"That would be lovely." Briar followed her aunt through the house. Briar opened the screen door and walked out onto the steps. Bonnie trotted along behind, wagging her tail happily. Hazel could only see a faint outline as she walked to the end of the garden.

She waited for the jug to boil, watching from the window. Her aunt always seemed to know what to do. Hazel, herself, had moments of confidence—usually at work. But mostly she still felt like she wasn't a proper adult. *At thirty-one*, she thought. How old do I have to be?

She pulled down the teapot from its shelf, glazed in brown to look like a ruru, the New Zealand morepork, with its sharp stare and tiny beak.

Her eyes fell on her laundry pile, overflowing in the corner, a grey nightie spilling over the edge of the basket. She couldn't even keep up to date with that. How was she supposed to take on an important role in the coven?

It stinks of cats out there, Bonnie said, coming back up the steps, and huffing down onto the wooden floor.

When Briar came in, Hazel put the teapot and two cups onto the kitchen table. "Close the door," she said, shivering a little. After turning the teapot three times, she poured out some tea and a raspberry smell rose up around her, immediately giving her comfort.

"Why *are* you so sure it should be me?" she said, when Briar sat down.

Her aunt didn't need to ask what she was talking about. But her look had some sympathy. "It's definitely you," she said, sipping at the tea.

That didn't really explain anything. "Does it have to be an empath?"

Briar opened her mouth to answer, then looked up.

"Don't need to greet your Grannie, is that it?" Emily swooped through the floorboards, hovering above Briar's head, long white hair hanging down.

"Sorry, Grannie," Briar said. "How's life?"

Emily chuckled. "Rude. Got a bit more grey in your hair, young one," she said.

"Oh, I know," Briar sighed. "I haven't been doing the charms, so it's starting to show through."

"Anyway, I heard a bit of your conversation," Emily said, with a smile. "If you have a big decision to make, you need to approach it from a scientific point of view."

Hazel nodded. Her Grannie used to work as a marine biologist, and she could normally be trusted to come up with a research-based and balanced approach. She thought Emily's advice would be to make a list of the pros and cons. That's how Hazel would approach a big decision at work. She could already think of at least three reasons to put in the negative column.

"Why don't you ask the runes?" Grannie Em said, instead.

"Well, this choice is not really up for debate," Briar said, coolly, narrowing her eyes at Hazel. "But why not? I know The Universe will be on my side."

Hazel followed Briar up the ladder and stood with her

head bent, below the sloped ceiling. Some warmth had been trapped in the attic from the sun. Briar was standing with her hands on the windowsill, looking at the view from the window, which Hazel herself never got sick of.

Without looking, she knew that beneath them were the window boxes and the porch covered in vines. To the right were the trees in all shades of russet and gold, and a corner of the boat at the bottom of Joel's garden. The land dropped away to dark green with the odd house down the valley.

"It pays not to forget that signs, portents and the moon are just as important as gravity or Occam's Razor." Grannie Em said. She spread out her cloth on the ground, and hovered over the floor, as limber as she ever was. Hazel sat down, legs crossed, opposite her, wishing she could float over the hard wooden floorboards.

Emily nodded in approval. "It's no small thing for Briar. But it affects you the most, after all, Hazel." She pulled out her old leather bag, and eased the drawstring open. Her mouth barely moved as she breathed a question into the opening. Then holding the bag gently, almost lovingly, she reached a silvery, white hand in and drew out a rune.

"Do you have to be so theatrical?" Briar asked, from beside the window.

"It's all part of it." Grannie Em snapped. She placed a rune in the middle. "This one represents you. It's The Man."

Hazel let out a laugh. But her Grannie just looked at her with her head on the side. "It means strength, or action. Bit old-fashioned, sure, but the witch runes are a very old method of fortune-telling. I think it suits you, Hazel. And it means that once you make up your mind, you'll follow through."

"This one is what supports you." She drew a rune and lay it below the other one. "The Eye. It is for focus, wisdom, truth, revealing. It can be what hurts."

"Alright, what favours you or helps you—The Blade." She

made a surprised noise. "This means sudden changes or endings. Or it can be cutting someone off." Hazel thought of Hadley, who she had cut off completely. That had definitely been good for her mental wellbeing.

Briar chuckled.

Her grannie's long white fingers turned a card over. "What is moving away? This one is The Woman. So it can mean Healing or Protection. I'd say that means that you're moving from being protected to taking more risks."

"That sounds about right," she said, thinking of having to protect the coven's magic book. She wondered what she would be at risk from, who would want to steal their family secrets.

"This last one on the right is what is coming towards you." Grannie Em bit her lip and scooped them all up into a pile, rather quickly. "I was never really any good at using the runes, anyway. Do you know who is though—"

"Grannie, what was the last one?"

"Oh, it was... just the blank one." She pressed her lips together, and dropped the tiles into the bag in twos and threes, carefully not looking at them.

"The Blank?" Briar sat up.

"What does that represent?" Hazel asked. "Grannie?"

"That's the void of all un-manifest potential," she said, in a falsely cheery voice, drawing the strings of the bag tight and shoving the runes under the pillow of the bed.

Her nightdress stayed perfectly still as she floated over to the windowsill.

"Well, I think we're all done here. If I was still alive, I would really want a good cup of tea and a bit of cake right now." She clapped her hands together, and although it made no sound, was a clear signal for the witches to go.

Once her aunt left, Hazel called Joel. "Sorry about that."

Turning on the jug, she made a cup of green tea and slid some bread into the toaster. She noticed the windows were fogged up, and gave them a quick wipe with a cloth, one-handed. The plants were drooping again, so she picked up the watering can and poured a dribble into each pot.

"That's fine," he said. "Who was that?"

"Just my aunt," she said. "Briar. She's Fritha's mum." Her toast came up with a pop and she smothered it with jam.

"Everything alright?"

"She was a bit concerned that the cottage is not as well protected as it could be," Hazel said, balancing the tea and toast as she walked into the lounge. "I feel like a bit of a sitting duck, really."

Hazel stretched out on the couch, munching on a piece of toast. She flapped a hand at Bonnie, who was staring at her food, a bubble of drool hanging from her jaw.

"Do you mean because the other witches might come back? But surely if we leave them alone, they'll leave us alone. They could have attacked us any time before now."

"Yeah, you're probably right," Hazel said, slowly. "Landlord rules apply now, don't they? Kirsten owns your property, so she can have access to the creatures when she wants. But she needs to give twenty-four hours notice before coming onto the property. And she is working through a property management company, anyway."

Then why have I got this feeling? But she didn't say that out loud, just flicked the crust to Bonnie, caught it with a snap.

"Would you be able to help me out with something tomorrow?"

"Sure," he said. "What is it?" He sounded a little suspicious, and thought for a second of teasing him that it was something witchy.

"I'm running a focus group at work tomorrow, but I don't

have enough people. You're not the exact target market, but you'll do."

"Oh, I will. Will I?"

"Yeah. Have a good sleep," she said, closing the curtains tight.

It was nerve-wracking waiting around here, doing nothing. That wasn't Hazel's style. She had to find out what was going on and stay one step ahead.

CHAPTER EIGHT

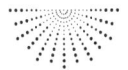

Hazel got caught up chatting to IT, so she was five minutes late to the focus group. She had logged and error first thing, and hadn't had access to the database all day. How did the Contact Team always manage to call back at the worst time?

"Sorry!" Hazel called, hurrying in. Tasha was standing by the door, and she passed the clipboard over with a long-suffering look on her face. About twelve other people were inside, filling out their forms.

At the far side of the room, a familiar face caught her eye. Joel looked up and grinned at her. It was good of him to come, even though it looked like lots of others had turned up.

"Hi everyone," she began. "This is a focus group about the flower festival. If you are here, it means you attended last year. All we need from you is your opinions, and we are very grateful for those. You will also get a—"

Hazel looked up straight into the face of Mandy. "Oh! Hello," she said. *What on earth was she doing here? Shouldn't Mandy be off selling people's houses out from under them?*

"Hi." Mandy said in a small voice, giving an embarrassed

half-wave. She passed her form back to Tasha, who tucked it into the folder.

"Hm, where was I up to?" Hazel looked down at the papers, idly flicking the page over, to avoid giving her an evil stare.

"Vouchers," Tasha said in a bored voice, adjusting the way her dark plait lay over her shoulder.

Hazel took a deep breath. "Everyone will get a grocery voucher for their participation. We will post them out shortly." She looked around, and a few people were nodding and smiling. "Okay, so where did you all hear about the festival?"

"Internet."

"My mum told me about it."

Hazel scribbled down the responses but hopefully Tasha was recording too.

I thought we'd get the voucher today. How am I supposed to buy my girlfriend a birthday cake?

The thoughts came from a tall man with curly blonde hair. Hazel rubbed her temples. Perhaps this had been a bad idea. She still couldn't control how many thoughts she heard from a group, and a faint headache was coming already.

"What do you think of these two logo designs?" Hazel asked, putting two pieces of paper on the table. She had made a few changes to Tasha's design.

"I like this one." Mandy pointed to the one on the left. Some others leaned forward, considering.

I'm only here to talk to people, came Mandy's thoughts. Hazel drew in a breath and fine tuned her telepathic abilities, reaching out carefully.

Someone from work got the invite and said I could get the voucher if I came. But I really just miss being around other people. How bloody sad is that!

I had some good friends back home. Sometimes, I wish... I have to be grateful to Kirsten though. Without her, I'd have nothing. She gave me confidence.

"Hazel! What were you going to ask next?" Tasha looked exasperated, as if she had asked her a few times.

"Can you do the next few questions?" Hazel asked and passed the clipboard over the table. "I have to get some air for a second."

She moved over to the window, opening it slightly. Today the air conditioning in the office was set to Antarctic, and the air from the window was just as cold.

But from there, she could watch Mandy, who looked just as embarrassed to be there as Hazel felt to see her there. She was chatting to the man next to her, who looked vaguely familiar.

He had wavy black hair, thinning in front, and he pushed back sometimes on his chair. It annoyed Hazel that she didn't know where she knew him from.

Imagine seeing Hazel here. Awkward. I was over at her place doing the summoning just a few days ago.

Hazel made herself keep looking down. The hairs on the back of her neck all raised up at the same time. She knew the candle and the carcass were part of something sinister. But a summoning? That was next-level magic.

Mandy pinned a chestnut curl up and looked across at her, thoughtfully. *Bet she's reading my mind right now.*

Hazel rubbed her hands together, trying to stop her fingers from trembling.

CHAPTER NINE

"I know, it's an ungodly hour for a Saturday." Bonnie was already awake, lying in a thin ray of sunshine, and her tail thumped on the floor as Hazel walked into the kitchen.

"You're up early," she said, reaching down to pat the dog's head.

So are you. What are you up to now?

"I'm going to figure out how to put some extra wards on the house," Hazel said. "What sort of a witch can't protect her own place?"

Does this have anything to do with that witch from yesterday?

Hazel tied her dressing gown up. She had to admit that it did. Mandy was unpredictable, like an ingredient bought off Covenslist. You were never quite sure what you'd get.

She opened her laptop and typed in 'house protection wards'. The instructions looked pretty basic, using salt, water and a compass. She could do this.

The sun was out but Hazel's bare feet were freezing in the dewy grass. Bonnie trotted along behind as she walked along the edge of the garden, checking her phone for the instructions as she went. She wondered what Joel would think if he looked over the fence now. Kooky. Crazy. Witch.

"That should do," she said, putting her hands on her hips. It felt a little better doing something.

A rustling noise in the tree made her search for a bird. Instead she saw glowing eyes, tucked in among the branches. She looked back quickly, heart beating fast, but nothing was there.

"Did you see that?' she whispered, but Bonnie was sniffing through the fence.

It's nothing, she told herself. *Get a grip, Redferne.* There had long been rumours of big cats in Otago and Canterbury, and the odd report from hunters in the hills. But the cottage was in the suburbs of the city.

She went inside, sat down and nestled her toes into her slippers. With a guilty look over her shoulder, took out a notebook. She wrote 'Suspects' at the top. No, that was too cliché. She crossed it out and wrote, 'People of interest'.

Mandy. She seemed to be the easiest of Kirsten's minions to investigate, but even then it wasn't going to be simple. Hazel had no idea how she was going to find out more about her. The British witch could sense other witches, so that meant she and Fritha couldn't follow her around.

She started out with something simple: Facebook stalking. She switched on the screen and chewed the edge off her thumb nail. What was Mandy's last name? She went into Jade's profile, and checked who had liked her photos.

There. Mandy had a simple profile, a smiling picture with a friend. The last updates were some pictures of June's party. Hazel looked closer, and saw herself on the edge of one such picture, looking very distracted. Oh Goddess, she was wearing a beanie!

Mandy's location still said the United Kingdom. She had 192 friends. Hazel quickly checked the list of four people who were their mutual friends, ticking them off. Jade, of course. June from work was on there. One was Pete, who Hazel had done a course with a long time ago. She should really take him off her friends list. The fourth one was Hadley.

You're talking to yourself, said Bonnie, from the floor. *Or should I say swearing to yourself.*

"Oh, right. Sorry."

Dunedin really was too small, sometimes. Hadley was her ex-boyfriend, the one who had taken everything she had, without giving anything back. He was the reason she had sworn off magic and men for years. How did Mandy know him?

Bonnie let out a grunt and rolled over onto her side. Hazel rubbed the furry tummy with her slippered foot absent-mindedly.

Did she really have to go and see Hadley and risk letting out all those feelings that she'd been running from? Surely, there must be another way.

Well, yes, you could give up sticking your nose into everyone else's business, she thought to herself.

A noise that sounded distinctly like a snort came from the dog.

No other solution came to her, so she found herself at the museum cafe on Monday, waiting for Hadley. It was a large, open space, and couldn't be construed as intimate by any stretch of the imagination. Good.

She stared out the window at the grass outside, covered in piles of soggy autumn leaves. Drips dropped from the trees onto the ground. A child was running towards the whisper dish, while his parent waited at the other one, ready to listen for the message. Hazel thought wryly that it was a good metaphor for being a witch. Sometimes she merely thought something and the whole coven knew.

Hadley spotted her and waved, but went to order a coffee first. He had a new black woolen coat and looked very professional, like one of the lecturers she saw around the university. He was wearing his hair differently now, too.

"Hi, Hazel." He sat down. "I ordered you a flat white." He showed his teeth, pleased with himself.

"Thanks." She frowned. That had always annoyed her, the way he assumed he knew what she wanted. "You've had a hair cut."

"Yeah," he said, ruffling his hair up. "So how have you been? What did you want to chat about?" He looked at his watch. "I haven't actually got long."

"Oh, nothing that important." She racked her brains about how to bring up Mandy. "What are you doing with yourself these days?"

"I'm doing my PhD part-time. Working too." He paused for a second to put his hand in his pocket. "Derek says hi." Hazel remembered how he always carried Derek, his rat familiar, everywhere with him. Ugh. She had forgotten that.

"Good on you." Hazel smiled a thin smile. "And hi to Derek. I'm still at the Council, but a bit higher up the, ah, food chain," she said, with a glance at where the rat's nose sniffed curiously.

He nodded, and took a sip of his long black.

"So how do you know Mandy?" she asked. *Oh Goddess*, she could be so blunt.

"Mandy?" He looked blank, then his expression cleared. "Oh, the English lady?"

"That's her." Hazel made sure to keep her voice even.

Hadley nodded. "Dunedin is too small, eh. Um, I think I bought something off her on Covenslist at first."

Covenslist was the witch network for second-hand goods.

Hazel had only looked at it a few times, as her family could usually source any magical things she needed. But she knew Hadley used it quite a lot, for getting potion ingredients that were hard to find here in Dunedin.

"We met up for a drink one night and that was pretty much it."

"Oh? Did you talk about anything interesting?"

"How do you know her, anyway?" He asked, and suddenly projected suspicion. Hazel reached out for his thoughts, but he must have been guarding them. "What's with all the questions?"

"Mandy's in my book club," she said. "She, uh, mentioned you."

"She did?" He lifted his head up and seemed to put his shoulders back a bit. "What did she say?"

Oh dear. Hazel knew that playing to his vanity would get him to open up. Now she had to think up something that Mandy had supposedly said about him.

"She said she was enjoying getting to know some really smart and funny people around the city." He wasn't actually that funny, but he thought he was. The lie tasted bitter in her mouth.

He smiled. "We had a good chat that night, actually. She had a pretty awful life in England, it sounded like. She had to get away."

"Did she?" Hazel asked, watching a harassed-looking teacher herd schoolchildren into a line near the stairs. They were getting distracted by all the colourful puzzles and toys in the gift shop.

"It was something about being unemployed for a long time," Hadley said, a thoughtful look on his face. "I might give her a call sometime."

"Just don't mention that I told you," Hazel put in quickly. "She'd be… embarrassed." This was bad. She was getting good at this. The problem with lying was that once you started, it was difficult to stop.

"She did offer me a free back wax but I never took her up on the offer," Hadley added, with a lift of his brow. "Don't know how you ladies do that stuff."

That was strange. Why would Mandy, a collections officer at the bank, offer him a free back wax?

"Does she moonlight as a beautician?" she asked.

"No, I think it was someone in her family," Hadley said. "Can't remember the name of the place but it was in Stuart Street."

"Shall we walk?" she asked, and Hadley pushed his chair back and stood up. They went up the stairs and curved around into the gallery. "So did she say anything else about why she came here?"

"I think she came for a fresh start. Her brother lives here and I'm sure she mentioned something about the trip giving her the confidence she needed."

"She's got a great job."

"In spite of how well she's doing, I don't think she's happy here. I know she has a daughter she didn't want to leave behind." Hadley stopped to read a panel about the Scottish settlers that came to Dunedin.

Hazel imagined Mandy with a teenage daughter, and found it hard to do. She couldn't be above forty.

"Much like these guys," Hadley added, pointing to the display. "Sometimes you have to go where the opportunities are. I guess they just trusted that one day they'd be reunited with their families."

"Mm," she agreed.

He looked up at her. "This is nice, Hazel," he said, lifting his arm as if to settle it behind her back. "Why don't we do this anymore?"

Because we broke up, she thought, dodging away. *A long time ago.*

They stopped near a glass case with a skeleton of a moa inside. It was a small species of the bird, extinct now in New Zealand. It was frozen in mid-peck. Hazel tried to ignore the group of school children watching a video, who were all thinking variations on 'I'm hungry'. The clock on the wall showed it was almost twelve.

Was he asking why she had cut him off? Placing her palm on the glass, she reflected. Because seeing him made her remember who she'd been at a different point in time. A black-and-white photograph of herself, she thought. Or a skeleton version that had not yet grown flesh.

"We used to have fun, but I think we've both moved on from there." She said it gently, but firmly, like she was disagreeing with someone in a work meeting. The truth was she didn't much like the person she was around him.

"Of course." He shook his head.

"It was nice to chat to you, though. Good luck with... everything." Hazel was surprised to find that she meant it. He had taken enough of her headspace, and now she was ready to move on.

CHAPTER TEN

This is on the way back to work, she told herself. *Not much of a detour at all.*

Hazel stepped over a puddle in the carpark. It had been raining all day, and didn't look like stopping anytime soon.

This had to be the right place. The pink sign wavered a little in the wind. Brows. It was the only beauty salon in the street. And it had a couple of eyebrows over the word. *Cute,* she thought.

What was she doing here? She turned back towards the street and then stopped.

Mandy doesn't have any other family here in New Zealand, she thought. *She has told me more than once how lonely she is. It has to be Kirsten who owns this place.*

She forced herself to face the salon, walked around to the window and peeked in. A man was sitting on a couch, flicking through magazines. She could see the edge of a black reception desk from there, but couldn't quite see who was behind it. It wasn't like Kirsten would be here right now anyway, was it? Surely, she wasn't actually a beauty technician? Just a silent partner or something?

Well, there was nothing for it but to go in. If she saw the other witch, she could make something up. It was better than doing nothing. She pressed on the handle and walked in, her footsteps echoing on the polished floors.

It looked like any other salon, white walls and lush couches with minimal furnishings. A shelf full of beauty products took up a whole wall, and some fake flowers in vases sat in the corner. Nobody was at reception, so she took a seat next to the man, smiling hello at him. The magazines were all from last summer, but she set one in front of her so she could look around.

Behind the reception desk was a price list, with names such as Dolphin Legs and Smoochable Upper Lip beneath the heading of Waxing. She reflected that 'Dolphin Legs' didn't quite convey the pain involved in getting the hairs pulled out by the roots. And dolphins didn't even have legs. Who was doing the marketing here?

She felt fortunate again that Fritha had come up with a potion to suppress hair growth. She supplied it to Hazel in return for tickets to council events. It was one easy lotion once a month, applied before a rainstorm, and she had been using it for the last ten years.

The receptionist came out—it wasn't Kirsten, but a young, black-haired woman. *Thank the Goddess.* Hazel went up to the desk, still not a hundred percent sure what she was going to say. She reached out and straightened up an empty basket that was on the desk.

"Hi, I'm Ha—" No, she couldn't give her real name. She added, "—ley." She cleared her throat. "Haley," she said again, with more confidence.

"Yes? How can we help?" The woman smiled at her. Hazel reached into her thoughts, tuning into the specific frequency of the woman's mind.

Please be someone interesting. It's going to be a really quiet afternoon.

"Um…" Hazel said, wracking her brains. "I was supposed to meet someone to look at purchasing some art for the salon. I'm an interior designer." She hoped that was interesting enough.

"Oh!" The woman looked surprised. "That's probably Kirsten. She's not here right now."

At the word Kirsten, Hazel felt a little thrill of excitement. Bingo! She'd followed the breadcrumbs, and it had paid off.

She didn't come in as we had so many cancellations, because of the weather. I'd rather be busy any day. One wax is all I've got to do this afternoon.

"Well, I could take a little look around and then send her an email. Five minutes." She held up her hand, with the fingers spaced apart. "She especially wanted me to look in her office, to, ah, check out the colours and the space."

"Her office?" The lady frowned. "If you just take a seat, I better ring her to check."

"No! Ah, don't bother her."

She felt a tap on her shoulder, and her heart jumped into her throat. She turned around slowly.

"Hi," Briar said. "Fancy seeing you here." Hazel's aunt was carrying a tray full of wrapped muffins, which she started putting into the basket on the desk, one at a time. They smelt amazing. "I'm just filling up the baking with some fresh goodies."

"Oh, good idea," Hazel said, a smile pasted on her face as she frantically thought of what to say. Her heart was beating in her ears and her face was hot. Her aunt had told her to keep her head down and stop sniffing around. She would be angry if she knew why Hazel was here.

But did Briar know who owned this place? She must have a contract to supply their baked goods.

Hazel cast around in her mind. "Um... Dolphin Legs!" she blurted. It was the first thing that came into her mind.

Briar laughed. "What?"

Hazel turned to the receptionist. "I'm getting the Dolphin Legs treatment."

"Ah... sure, I can fit you in shortly." The woman behind the desk raised her eyebrows a little but was evidently satisfied that sampling the services of the salon was just part of the design process.

"Okay. See you later—" Briar said.

"Yep. Bye," Hazel said, quickly before her aunt could say her name. Picking up the tray and walking back out to the door, Briar gave one last look over her shoulder as she went out into the rain.

As Hazel was lying on the table staring at the white ceiling, she reflected that it was lucky the weather was so bad. They would never have been able to fit her in otherwise.

She snuggled into the heated towels beneath her, relaxed now that she knew she wasn't going to be caught by her aunt or anyone else. The towels were warm and the soft music gave her a false sense of security. *Relax,* they told her, *you're in safe hands.*

What was she thinking anyway, coming here, going undercover? Hazel didn't know where she was meant to look, or what she was looking for. She needed a new plan.

The beauty technician opened the door quietly and walked over to the bed.

"You hardly need it, sweetie," the woman said, looking over her legs sticking out below the towel, "but we can give it a go, anyway."

Hazel gritted her teeth, as the beauty technician leant in close and pressed the wax down. She studied the ceiling, the recessed lights and plain white paint, finished quickly and sloppily in the corners where it met the wallpaper.

"And breathe out," the woman said. She smiled, and tore the wax off. Hazel cursed her aunt with every screaming pore of her skin.

CHAPTER ELEVEN

Hazel itched to get back to the beauty salon, but as it turned out, she couldn't do any sleuthing the next day.

It was warm in the office, and she stared at the flower festival copy until the words blurred to grey on the screen, and she had to blink her eyes to keep them open. Why was the air conditioning always set to the wrong temperature?

Her phone vibrated on the desk with a text message. 'Full moon tonight. The usual place.' It was from her mum. She locked the screen and looked around to see if anyone was watching. Tonight must be her initiation ceremony. She paused, heart racing, her finger over the ring symbol. Should she call her mother and ask what would happen?

Her office phone emitted a discordant ring and she jumped. "Someone is at Customer Services for you," said Bev, in a flat voice.

Hazel sidled past the desks, feeling frustrated. She didn't have time for this. The morning had been spent at a course, organised by her boss, to learn how to use the calendar function of their email software properly. She was sick of hearing 'work smarter', 'efficiency', and 'automate'.

From the thoughts of everyone else in the team, they all felt the same about the course. It was supposed to save her time, but they had travelled to the other side of the city to do the training. What about *that* lost time? And now she only had two hours to get her work done.

"Oh," Hazel said, flushing, as she came around the divider. Joel was waiting on one of the grey chairs, and he sprang up when she spoke.

"I just wanted to drop this off," he said, passing her a Tupperware. "You said you had a course on today and the free lunch might not be very good."

"Thanks. That's so kind," she said. Hazel opened the lid to see a piece of chicken resting on some roast vegetables inside.

"Make sure you heat it up." He ran a hand through his hair. She thought that the display of affection made him feel a bit awkward.

"I will," she said, warmth spreading through her and settling somewhere in her chest. "It was finger food, so I'm starving right now."

Joel came closer, and she could see the stubble below his lower lip. "And I want to cook you dinner tomorrow night, Red. Save you from your tinned soups."

He'd never called her Red before and it seemed like it slipped out by mistake. He put his hand lightly on the small of her back, and she studied his mouth, wanting to be drawn closer, but stuck in place.

She was conscious of Bev standing behind the desk. With one of the biggest gossips in the office less than two metres away, Hazel wasn't going to do anything more than look.

Then after, he thought, eyes burning into her. *I want to start by peeling off —*

"That sounds great," she said loudly, slipping out of his grasp. "I'm busy tonight so I'll see you tomorrow."

She rushed past Bev, who was pretending to work, and stopped to fan her face around the corner.

When Fritha picked her up in her little electric car after work, the wind was scattering leaves in the street. Hazel was thinking fondly of her couch filled with soft cushions at home.

Instead, they had eaten burgers from their wrappers while heading out of town. Later, they sang boy band songs at the top of their voices as they wound their way up the coast.

Hazel wasn't sure why the coasts made the best spots for magic, but she guessed it had something to do with the blending of different elements.

"Are you going to be alright like that?" Fritha asked, eyeing the heels and work skirt she was wearing, as they stepped out of the car in the parking area.

They set out on the path to the headland. The clay had eroded with the power of the water, so in some places, a narrow bridge was all that still remained of the land. Waves crashed into huge blow holes filled up by the incoming tide. She slipped a little, and Fritha asked if she was alright.

"I'm fine," she said, turning to her friend, curious to see how much Fritha knew about the ritual. "What about you? You don't mind… "

"Oh, definitely not. You have it." Fritha pushed her hands away as if it was something she wanted to get rid of. "Mum said it's like being the kid chosen to organise their parent's funeral."

Hazel made a face. That sounded just great.

"Do you know what is going to happen?" she called, the wind whipping her hair around her face.

Fritha shrugged.

It was cold on the Huriawa Peninsula, but every other time she appreciated the beauty of the place. A great fortress had once stood there, and it was still a place of power, a headland covered in grass and open to the buffeting wind, which cut through the material of her blouse. The sea below was dark, with whitecaps.

Hazel stood at the edge. In front of them was a tiny cauldron. She didn't know what that was for, and it seemed as if her aunt wanted it that way. She couldn't see a book anywhere.

Briar and Moira were already there, sitting on cushions with a blanket around them. Briar held the edge of the blanket open and Fritha sat down. "Might as well be comfortable, eh? There's room for you two in here."

"I made some extra wards for the cottage," she said to Briar, kneeling down. "Just to be safe. But I'm not sure that they're working."

"They should be," Briar answered. "At some point, you have to trust the magic. Did you walk the perimeter while placing them?"

"Yes, around the fenceline. And I used a compass to make sure they pointed towards the proper directions."

"Did you charge them first?"

"Oh no, I didn't. Damn," There was a lot to think about as a proper part of the coven again. Sometimes Hazel felt like she was back at school. "So, um..." She trailed off.

Briar smiled at her. "Try not to worry. When your mum and dad get here, we can get started."

Hazel felt their arrival before she saw them as a comfortable feeling clicked into place around her breastbone. Aster took her own time to get places, preferring to get there 'when she was needed, not when she was invited'. She was walking confidently along the pathways, Harold coming along behind in his cap, holding the bags.

"Mum, Dad, how are you guys?"

"*We're* fine." Her mum came up and hugged her, and a faint scent of herbs reached Hazel. "Are you alright?" she asked.

"Yes." Hazel looked off to where the moon was rising over the peninsula.

Harold took some herbs from the bag and ripped them up, adding them to the cauldron. He collected rocks and placed them in a circle, then laid sticks over top.

"Not long to wait." Aster passed around some fudge. "Your dad made this," she said. Hazel took a large piece and held it in her mouth, feeling the sugar dissolve on her tongue and turn to creamy goodness. For her dad, making food was his way of showing love.

Hazel looked out over the dark water, wishing she could climb down and swim in blessed cool and quiet. She could just make out the Matanaka Peninsula, where the oldest farm buildings in New Zealand were tiny little squares against the skyline. Soon enough, the moon was round and full in the sky.

"There's something I didn't mention, Hazel," Briar said. "Once the ceremony is done, I'll be out of it straight away." She struck a long match and lit the sticks on fire. "You'll be It from then on."

"What do you mean?" Hazel hissed. She had hoped for a gradual transition. "You never told me that. Why do you need to do this anyway? You're a fantastic Keeper, and you're only 40." She was babbling but she didn't care. It was one thing not to be prepared but she hadn't been told anything.

"I'm almost 43." Hazel saw the lines on Briar's face, small ones near the eyes around the mouth. "And it is not because I'm going to pass away or anything. It's just the right time." She smiled reassuringly at Hazel and patted her arm. "Now, I was told that when someone else gets the seal, I will forget absolutely all the knowledge I had from it. I'll be fine... just a little less." Her aunt's skin was pale, almost translucent, and Hazel wanted to cry.

"You'll be *more*," she said to Briar. "Because you have passed the book on and made the sacrifice for the good of the coven."

"Yeah, that's right, love," said Moira. "She has a good point. Smart one, this one."

"Book?" Briar asked, drawing her eyebrows together, but waved her hand as if it didn't matter. "Well, it is time."

Aster stood up and took a deep breath and her face was lit by the glow from under the cauldron. "We're meeting tonight to bring in a new Secret Keeper," she said. "Over to you, Briar."

The others looked up and slowly moved to take their places in a circle. Hazel slipped off her shoes and stepped into the middle. If she was going to take part in a magic ritual, she was going to be comfortable.

"Hazel Redferne. Descended from the witches of Redferne," Briar said. "You'll be our reference. Our grimoire. Our wise one."

Hazel clenched and unclenched her fists, feeling very watched.

"I send the energy of our forebears into this vessel." Briar held something small in her hands. Hazel couldn't quite see what it was.

She stepped closer to Hazel and opened her hands up to show a tiny locket. Briar reached towards her and plucked some hair from her head, dipped it into the cauldron, spinning it quickly into a ball to fit it into the locket.

"I think one hair would have been enough," Hazel grumbled, but nobody heard her because the magic had started.

The moonlight lit the headland with a bright silver glow. Thin tendrils of light snaked along the ground towards the middle of the circle and around the outside. Briar took her lock of hair from the locket and threw it on the ground. Hazel and Briar stood still in the centre as the light glowed beneath their feet, the locket between them.

"Only one can keep the vow. I relinquish my knowledge to the coven."

Her aunt closed her eyes to concentrate and the others repeated the words. The magic tendrils wrapped around Briar's arms and legs, and Hazel saw they were pulling gently, massaging her joints. The light crept over to where the hair had fallen and sparks fizzled along it, like the end of a sparkler.

"Pick up the locket, love," Aster said. "Put it on."

Hazel lifted the chain over her head, and let the locket settle against her breastbone. The metal warmed immediately and a buzzing sensation climbed her legs and body.

Briar faced her. "Will you never tell a soul what you are?"

She nodded.

"Do you agree to keep the knowledge given to you secret?" Briar asked. She had to raise her voice over the wind.

"Will you only use your knowledge for the good of the coven?"

Hazel nodded again. Her wrists and elbows were getting uncomfortable, and she wanted to rip the magic from her, like it was a blood pressure monitor in the doctor's clinic that had gone rogue. It squeezed and pressed, as if it would never stop. Was something being tattooed on her skin?

Just as she thought she couldn't bear it any longer, the pressure was gone as quickly as it came. A feeling of peace came over her, and she felt as if she could sleep for several days.

Briar stumbled forward and put her hand on Hazel's shoulder to steady herself. She had tears streaming down her face.

"Are you alright?" Hazel asked.

"Yes. Are you?" Briar said. She wiped the tears away. "I'm not even sure why I'm crying."

"Did it work?" Moira asked, rushing forward to put her arm around Briar.

Hazel looked down at her arms which were bare, but a bright red. "I don't know."

"It did," Briar said simply, scrubbing at her cheeks with her shirt. "But that is just the beginning, dear."

Hazel felt stupid, like her mind was loping along a few moments behind reality. "So there's no book?" she asked, but Briar didn't hear.

Aster came over to Hazel, and applied something to her wrists. "It's just an aloe vera ointment. To help with the burning."

"Thanks, Mum." As long as she remembered, her mother had been making salves, poultices and tinctures from plants. Even before Hazel knew there was a problem, Aster would apply something cool on the inside of her elbow or to the bottom of her foot. A steady stream of people came to the family house in Oamaru, went into the little shed with her mother, and left soon after clutching a small jar or bag of herbs.

"And you, Briar," Aster said, motioning to her sister to put her palms face up. "That must be a huge loss for you. It's fine to shed a tear or two."

"It's done now," her aunt said in a low voice.

Hazel didn't want to say that she didn't feel any different. She wondered what would happen if it hadn't worked. What if she wasn't in fact the right person? What if the knowledge was lost forever?

CHAPTER TWELVE

Sleep came easily that night, and Hazel felt as if her eyes had barely closed when the alarm went off. She was rubbing them when Joel brought the car around in front of the cottage.

"Are you still half asleep?" he called, grinning, when she came to the door.

"I got dressed, at least." *Perhaps not quite enough, though,* she reflected, as she stepped outside and the freezing wind sliced through her, leaving goose pimples in its wake.

"What did you get up to last night?" Joel grabbed her and pulled her in close.

"Witch— ah, family stuff." She longed to tell him about the ceremony; the worry, the pain and her fear that she somehow wasn't good enough to be the Secret Keeper. But she knew she couldn't. "I didn't get home til almost ten."

"Are you too tired for dinner tonight? Made by me?"

"No way," she said. "You're not getting out of it that easily."

Hazel's morning didn't improve much at work. She had trouble concentrating so she spent the lunch hour out walking in the freezing air to stay awake.

She walked down Princes Street, past cafes and hotels, a takeaway shop and some abandoned shopfronts. Hazel crossed the road and wandered through The Exchange, the bricked square surrounded with office buildings. The Stock Exchange used to stand there but had been demolished some fifty years previously.

A buzzing came from her bag, and she reached down to answer her phone.

"Hello?" As she straightened up, a jolt of déjà vu hooked Hazel behind the eyelids. She looked carefully around, trying to see what had spurred the feeling.

On her left, the Cargill Monument cast a long shadow over her path. She had walked through the square before, but never stopped there for anything that she could remember. John Wickliffe House, a low concrete building with a glass front, was straight ahead. A few concrete planters and a bench seat sat in front of it. It all looked just the same as it always had.

"Hazel?" Joel was saying. "You there?"

"Sorry, I'm… okay. What did you want?"

"Are you sure? I just asked if you'd get me a couple of ingredients for tonight. I thought I had some garlic but it's gone a bit brownish. I need three cloves. And a packet of spaghetti. I haven't got enough left."

Hazel laughed to herself. It sounded as if he was going to cook her that flatter favourite, spaghetti bolognese. At least he was using real garlic, not just adding a tin of ready-made sauce to the pasta.

"Of course," she said. "I'll see you soon." She took one last look around the square in hopes of any clues, before taking out a pen to write the ingredients on her hand. Any home-cooked food had to be better than another meal of soup or noodles.

Hazel dropped off her bag at home and Bonnie followed her through the gate to Joel's house.

"You're here," Joel said, coming out onto the deck and reaching for the ingredients. She smiled when she saw him with tomato sauce splatters on his shirt. "Now just wait out here for a second. I'll be with you in just a moment." He lifted a finger and held it there for a moment, undecided.

Oh, how cute, she thought. *He's nervous.*

Yeah, he is, Bonnie said, flopping down on the grass on her side. A white cabbage moth fluttered around them, but the dog couldn't even be bothered trying to chase it.

Hazel nudged Bonnie with her foot, looking around at the section. Joel had let the grass grow and there were clumps of daisies growing in it. The pittosporums bulged out, wild and woolly, their evergreen tops curling over, waving in the breeze.

"Okay, you can come in now," Joel said. "Dinner won't be for a while so I thought we could watch a movie."

"Sounds good," she said.

His phone made a ding noise and he looked down at it. "Oh, sorry, I hate these things."

"What?"

"I made an Instagram post like you told me to," he said. "I got one of my customers to send a photo of themselves with one of my chests. Now I'm getting all these notifications when someone likes it—it's bloody annoying."

She laughed. "That reminds me of the joke about how you can tell a bad marketer."

"How?"

"They're anti-social," she said.

He just stared at her.

"Not funny?" she asked. "It's because... you have to get into social media with marketing these days, and… oh, never mind.

That's a good thing, though, about the likes. You can turn the notifications off if you want."

"Later. Anyway, I thought we could watch a classic—*The Shining*."

"Ooh, the one with Jack Nicholson?"

His eyes widened. "You're into horror movies?"

"My aunt made me watch all the old ones. But I love that, I'll definitely watch it again." Thinking of Briar made her wonder how her aunt was, after the ceremony. She resolved to message her later. "I'm so glad you didn't choose some rom com."

He shook his head and lined up the movie on his phone. Today, he had folded away the little table so that the wooden bench seat had an unobstructed view to the flatscreen television. He reached underneath the windows and pulled out some long cushions from the cupboard.

"Your seat." She sat down and was surprised to find it was as comfortable as any couch and soon snuggled into the cushion.

He reached up and shut the curtains. "It's just for atmosphere," he assured her, but his grin said otherwise.

He plopped down beside her and put his arm around her shoulders. It was heavy and warm, and as she watched, she managed to forget about the coven responsibilities and the other witches.

After the film, he folded out the little table. A loud, rumbling noise gurgled in the silence.

"Sorry, I'm starving." she said, with a smile.

"Good." Joel went over to serve up two plates, setting one in front of her and one in front of him. She gasped, shocked.

It was a meal fit to be served in any high class restaurant. Prawns nestled among the strands of pasta, with wilted spinach and capsicum and tomatoes providing colourful touches.

"It's spaghetti with prawns and slow-roasted tomatoes," he said, lifting an eyebrow. "Wine?"

"Yes please." She used her knife to taste the sauce. The tang of the tomato blended with a hint of rich garlic and black pepper. "This is…"

Okay, maybe she had under-estimated him. Definitely.

"This is amazing," she said, taking a mouthful. "I really thought… "

"You thought I'd be a shit cook?"

"Yeah, sorry," she said, hanging her head. "I sort of did. I'm not sure why," she said.

He hunched over and ate the rest of his meal quietly, only responding to her questions with one-word answers.

People have underestimated me my whole life, he thought. *I just didn't think you would.*

"Sometimes I just don't have the energy to be everyone's therapist." Hazel cuddled into Bonnie back at the cottage. She had left after dinner, letting herself quietly through the gate and unlocking the door to the cottage. "I do feel bad."

Bonnie stared solemnly back. *I'm always happy to be yours*, she said.

"You are the best dog," she said, and Bonnie wagged her tail against the sofa with a soft thump. "It is just too much, sometimes. I hear everything everyone is thinking. Some people are so sad, and some are really horrible. I'm not *enough* to help everyone. It never stops."

"Oh yeah, I brought some work home." Her eyes fell on the pile of papers from work and she scrambled up to take a closer look. Sifting through the file, she pulled out the forms from the focus group. She had brought them home to address the envelopes.

On the top of the pile was Amanda Kennett. Of course. A little thrill of fear and excitement ran through her as she realized what that meant. Everyone had added their addresses, so they could receive their vouchers. Now she knew where Mandy lived.

CHAPTER THIRTEEN

A few days later, Hazel walked through the front door of a little house in Corstorphine, a smile on her face in case anyone was watching. It always paid to look confident in whatever you did, especially when your heart was banging inside your chest.

It smelt nice inside Mandy's house, like baking bread, or maybe pastry. Hazel closed the door behind her carefully, trying to look like a kindly relative going to feed the cat. It was just a simple spell to get in, she had found it on the witch web. What was she doing inside someone else's house? Was she a criminal now?

No, she thought. She was just a person trying to protect her coven and her boyfriend. She had to find out what Kirsten was up to and it was going to be easiest to find out through her sister-in-law, Mandy. It would be in and out, nice and easy.

She walked quickly through the house, looking in doors for a bedroom or study. The house was small but tastefully decorated, with bright touches of cyan or mustard against minimalist white furniture. Here was the bedroom, with a large king size bed and a bright blue throw. The bedside table had two drawers, and she pulled the top one out carefully. It contained old foundations, blushers and night creams.

She pulled a little too hard on the bottom drawer. It came right out and papers fell onto the floor. They were in a manilla folder marked Visa Application. Hazel hurriedly tidied them back up and stuffed them in the drawer, peeking over the bed at the empty driveway.

She went back out of the room and looked into the next room along the hallway, which looked to be a sewing room. It had one small window, a huge desk and piles of fabrics of all colours folded and stacked into bright slabs. Hazel checked the drawers which were filled to the brim with cottons, zips and domes and ran her fingers over a fabric box that was sitting on the floor beside the sewing machine case.

Lifting the lid off, she saw Mandy's own face, framed in those chestnut curls, staring out at her. It was a photograph of her and a blonde, smiling child reaching for an ice cream. Hazel's heart clenched. This was her daughter? Why would she have left this beautiful child behind?

Underneath was a piece of green paper. *In exchange for a year of your life—*

The door creaked and slammed into its frame. Hazel turned to see Mandy, standing in front of the door.

"I never suspected you to be this type of person." Mandy looked genuinely hurt, as she turned to face her. "I thought we might even be friends eventually."

Friends? She had summoned something at Hazel's house. Was she delusional? Hazel searched wildly for some reason to be there.

"I'm just looking for—"

"Don't even bother," Mandy said, disgusted. "You've got a picture of my wee girl in your hand. You snuck into my house while I was out and went through my things. It's just lucky I forgot my lunch today. Then when I came in the door, I could sense magic straight away."

Her hands curled into fists. "What do you want?"

Hazel knew she could make people tell her things. Her only chance was to ask her straight out and see if she could get any information.

"Why are you doing things for Kirs—?" She blurted out at the same time as Mandy grunted and lunged towards her.

She was quick and small, and Mandy ducked under her arm and blocked her, while knocking her foot out from under her. It didn't quite knock her down, but Hazel was off balance and that was enough. Mandy was able to push her down and she fell hard onto her bottom. Was this woman trained in martial arts?

"She's my sister-in-law," she said. "As I told you." She was breathing heavily, and didn't seem to want to talk. "She offered me a lot to come here and help her out. You don't know her, it's what she does."

She stood over Hazel, deciding what to do next.

"What did she offer you?"

"My daughter," she said simply.

"But your daughter lives with someone else now?"

Mandy took a couple of steps towards the door, opening it up quickly and stepping through it. "With her dad." The words were blurted quickly through the gap, before the door shut and the key turned in the lock. Her voice came from the other side. "I'm just going to leave you in there for a bit while I think of what to do."

Where was the bit of paper with the spell on it to unlock the door? Hazel searched her pockets, but it must have fallen out. She stood up and tugged at the window, which appeared to be painted shut, then watched helplessly as Mandy walked down the driveway, leaving her alone and trapped.

She wouldn't be missed at work, because she had taken the day off. To tidy up the garden, she had told the others.

Joel thought she was in the office, and even Bonnie had no idea where she was.

She settled down against the side of the desk to wait.

When the shadows lengthened against the door, Hazel heard someone outside the window. Perhaps Mandy would have Kirsten with her.

She heard the front door open and shut.

"Are you alright, Hazel?" Mandy's voice reached her, panicked.

"Yes, she called, standing up and brushing off her clothes.

"Good." She seemed to be a bit calmer then. "I'm not going to talk about it with you. Because I know you can read minds. And... I'm not ready to discuss it."

"I understand. Can you let me out though?"

"Oh dear, this isn't very good at all, is it?" Mandy paused, and said in a quieter voice. "I will let you out soon. I'm not a monster."

"Of course you aren't." She leaned against the wooden door. "I'd probably do the same if you were inside my house, to be honest. Bonnie would never let that happen, though. Don't you have a familiar?"

"I used to, back in England. She was the cutest little grey squirrel, and she went anywhere without being noticed. Natty was a wonderful familiar, but didn't really have any street smarts. We think she ate some rat poison."

"Oh, that's awful." She meant it. It was always difficult when a familiar bond was broken, and it could sometimes take years until a new familiar showed up. Bonnie was Hazel's first real familiar and she couldn't imagine how it would feel if anything happened to her.

"I'm going to go get a cup of tea, alright?" Mandy asked.

"Would you just wait with me for a while?"

She heard Mandy sigh. "I suppose I can." After a minute, she tapped a finger on the wood and said. "She's a *good* person, you know."

"What sort of tea are you having?"

Hazel knew she would be able to hear Mandy's thoughts through the door soon. If she could only keep her talking.

"Earl Grey's my poison. What's yours?"

"I'm quite partial to peppermint or raspberry. But each has their uses, don't they?"

"That they do."

"Would you get me some water?"

"Um… " Mandy wavered, thinking about how inhumane it would be if she declined. Hazel chose her moment to ask and hoped that Mandy wouldn't be able to resist answering with the truth.

"What are you waiting for anyway? Why not let me out?"

Where are they? They should be here by now.

Her coven. Hazel went cold all over, but forced herself to keep talking.

"So, uh, why are you here in New Zealand?" Hazel reached out through the wood, desperately searching for her thoughts, seeking for the truth.

I needed a fresh start, with the confidence Kirsten gave me. I'm only here for a year or two then I'll go back to my daughter.

"You're doing it now, aren't you?" Mandy sounded outraged. Hazel heard a beeping sound and muffled voices as Mandy walked away with the phone.

Her heart sped up. She tried the door again, and wracked her brains to remember the unlocking spell. She had to get out of here.

She breathed slowly, deliberately, forcing herself to be calm. Bonnie. Of course. She had to get a message to her familiar. But there was no way Bonnie would be able to run here all the way from Mornington, even before she had her broken leg.

Although her connection was good, it was a long distance to send. And Hazel's legs were shaking, despite her efforts to relax.

Bonnie. I'm in trouble. I'm locked in a house. Send Joel. She bent over, leaning against the door, sending it over and over again, not knowing whether it got through. Would Joel even come? He seemed pretty angry with her when they were together last.

"Not long to wait," Mandy called. "They are car-pooling. Someone's kid hung onto them and wouldn't let them leave. Wouldn't you know it?" She heard the footsteps going away.

But something else was coming to her. *Put your ear close to the lock. The spell is 'Pieces of metal, holding fast, Tell me your secrets from when you were cast.'*

Bonnie was such a good dog. The best dog, in fact. Hazel listened to the locking mechanism and chanted the words under her breath, cringing every time she spoke in case the woman outside heard. She sent some magic into the keyhole, probing, listening. She heard a faint click. She tried the doorknob and it turned.

The next part had to be quick. She pushed the door open hard, in case Mandy was standing outside and lunged into the hallway. The door banged against the wall and sprang back. But Mandy wasn't there. Hazel walked down the hallway silently, looking into doors. It was too quiet. She turned around and saw Mandy behind her.

"What—"

Hazel panicked. She had never been in a situation like this before. As the pulsing of her blood grew louder in her ears, she remembered a simple spell she had learned as a child to get rid of bullies.

"Zits!" She said, and pushed her magic forward in a wave. She couldn't bear to look.

There was a sort of slumping noise, and she opened one eye to see Mandy lying on the floor, red spots dotted across her face and chest.

Damn, she thought. Of course, her magic would be stronger now. All of her first aid courses went out of her head. Pulse, should she check that? She put two fingers to her neck and felt a steady thrum thrum.

Just then a tap came at the door. Hazel tried to walk, but it was as if her feet were frozen in place. The door opened and Joel crept in, with Bonnie looking out from behind him.

"What the—" he mouthed.

She breathed out, and they stared at each other for an instant. "Park the car around the corner," she managed. "I can't seem to move."

CHAPTER FOURTEEN

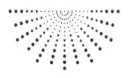

They had been hauling for what felt like forever. Hazel looked up, getting a better grip on the ankles. "What's the safest place to hide a body?"

He had wrapped her in a warm hug, that slowly thawed her fright, rubbing her back over and over. She was so grateful that he'd come, in spite of everything. And she told him so over and over.

"That's alright," he said. "It's alright."

As the feeling came back into her fingers and toes, she realized they had to hurry. She shook herself off and forced her legs to move.

Now Joel's mouth was set in a determined line. He grunted as he picked Mandy up with his hands in her armpits and walked back a few steps into the bedroom.

He gently lowered her down. "Go on then."

"On the second page of the search results."

He laughed, in spite of himself. She thought it might be shock.

"Because nobody ever looks there," she said.

"Yeah, yeah, I see," he said in a loud whisper, picking her up again. "Who is this, anyway?"

"It's Mandy, the witch I told you about. She's a relative of your lovely landlady and part of her scheme. She's going to be completely fine. We just have to get out of here as quick as we can. Come on, last push."

They settled Mandy on the bed and pulled a quilt over her. She looked like she was sleeping soundly, albeit with a few acne spots on her face. Hazel leaned close beside her ear and sent healing thoughts into her. She would wake up a bit sore but otherwise fine.

A car pulled into the driveway and they heard the sound of doors opening. They stared at each other for a second and then ran for the back door, and slipped through just as the front door was closing.

In the car, Joel was quiet. "I'm pretty sure I'm an accessory to a crime."

Hazel grimaced. "It wasn't ideal. I never meant her to find me. But they are the ones who sold your house from under you, hurt me and my dog, and locked me up in a room all day. It's not like it was unprovoked."

"Should we talk to the police? We should. Shouldn't we?"

"And say what? That we broke into someone's house and assaulted them because they are working for a witch?" She kept her voice low and calming. "It was a stupid zit spell that popped into my head from nowhere. Her skin will be greasy for a few weeks but that's about it. No, we can't tell them. How did you know to come and find me anyway?"

"I heard barking outside and your dog was sitting outside my door. She wouldn't stop until I came out. Then she went over to the car and barked some more. When I opened the door, she jumped in and sat there, in the front seat. She… navigated by pointing her nose."

"Clever!" Hazel reached over and patted her, sneaking a glance out the back at the same time, but the road behind was clear.

Yeah, what were you doing without me? Bonnie said to her. *You know I hate barking. It's demeaning.*

"Are you afraid of them coming after us?" Joel asked, as they drew near to the cottage.

"Yes," she said, simply.

He changed the gears, and Hazel cringed at how loud the car was in the quiet suburb.

"Come over to my place. We can listen to some music, maybe watch some trash reality tv."

"I'll be there in just a moment," she said. First, she had to prepare some healing, calming tea. They both needed it.

CHAPTER FIFTEEN

The next morning, Hazel sat down at the table in her kitchen, with a crossword. She was determined not to think about what had happened at Mandy's house. Bonnie was snoring in a patch of sunshine at her feet.

"Present transport," she murmured, taking a gulp of chamomile tea. "What could that mean?"

Spiky thoughts of breaking into the house crept into her head. What was she coming to? Just because Joel had been treated badly, did that mean she should stoop to their level?

She dotted the pen on the paper. How else was she going to protect her coven? And her and Joel?

Hazel heard a buzz and waved her hand with the pen in it around absentmindedly. *It's crossword time*, she thought, gritting her teeth against the intrusive thoughts. "I present to you. I introduce…"

She swatted at the fly, but it still buzzed around her.

"Present. That could be a gift, donation. Or it could mean now, today," she mused. She opened the window to let it fly out, and Bonnie sat up with a start, head cocked to the side.

Now that she looked at it, it looked more like a bee, from

its yellow stripes. Hazel grabbed a section of the paper to shoo the bee out.

"It could be a sleigh. Like for transporting presents."

Bonnie jumped up, snapping her jaws.

I can't seem to catch it! Bonnie lunged against the wall. Another hum joined the first one.

"Get out!" She called, waving the stack of paper. The paper went right through the bees and they continued to buzz angrily, up towards the window and back down.

A noise like an engine came towards her and she saw a whole swarm of them heading for the window. Hazel's blood ran cold.

She slammed the window shut. *Ghost bees. Zombie bees. What the—*

Hazel summoned her magic from within. She pushed her hands outwards and sent the largest push of energy she could. It was weak. Not enough. She didn't have the strength after last night.

But Bonnie was watching. She jumped and landed hard with all four paws on the ground, letting out a little whine when her still-healing leg jolted. She was magnifying the magic, drawing on their connection to act as a prism and focus the energy outwards. A surge of power rippled under Hazel's feet.

The bees hit the invisible shield and boomed off, zapping away into the distance.

Hazel was breathing hard. "That was awesome. Thank you," she said. The dog put her front paws out, and rolled onto her back.

It was easy to forget Bonnie was a powerful magical being, when she was rolling around on her back with her paws in the air, jaws gaping in an upside down grin. Hazel tickled the scratchy fur on Bonnie's belly just near the front leg joint.

Hazel reflected that perhaps this was the Threefold Rule

coming back to bite her. But what on earth were undead insects swarming on the house for? And how did they get past the wards?

Someone sent them, Bonnie said. *Be ready for more.*

This was exactly the sort of thing the wards were supposed to protect against. And she had added extra protection too. Unless something was destroying the guard spells as fast as they could make them.

"Grannie!" she called, heading for the attic, and shimmying up the ladder as fast as she could.

"Have you got that book here?" Hazel asked, when she popped her head into the attic.

"You mean *The Menagerie*? Oh yes, I love that one." Hazel had left it with her grannie, since she took so much joy from reading it. Emily went over to the desk and pulled it out of the row of books.

"Oh Goddess, it's probably overdue by now," Hazel said, biting her lip. "Because it's so old, the lady in Souls of Scrolls said I could only borrow it. I'd buy it if I could."

"Mm," Grannie Em said, running her hand down the bound green cover. "It really is beautiful."

"Listen, Grannie, we just had an attack of zombie bees. Zom-bees, I'm going to call them. I got rid of them, it's alright," she said, quickly, when her grannie's eyes widened. "But I need to look something up. Is there any sort of creature that could be summoned to destroy protection charms?"

"Let me see, dear," her grannie said, opening the book and placing one long whitish finger on the page, with maddening slowness.

Hazel sat down on the bed, which had a fine layer of dust

on the old-fashioned white linen. "You should really dust up here, Grannie," she said.

Emily waved her words away. "If there's one thing I shouldn't have to do when I'm dead, it's that."

Her long silvery hair fell over the page. "So, under Protect, we have… Demons that protect, protection familiars, protective behaviour, spirit guides, spirits that protect graves… Aha! Creatures that feed off protection charms."

Her grannie glided along the floorboards, holding the book in her arms. "This is a large cat, black or brown, which can be summoned to hunt the protective charms of a certain magical being. It feeds off the wards, slowly getting more powerful as it consumes them. It will not stop until it has consumed all of the target being's magical wards. Does that sound right?"

Hazel considered for a moment. Normally, the back yard was full of stray cats, circling her legs, scratching on tree branches, or squinting at her from the fence. But lately, there had been a distinct lack of feline company. Maybe something was scaring them off.

"Yes, it does." *A large cat.* She remembered the eyes glowing from the darkness in the trees that night, and shivered.

She'd had a few feelings that things were 'off' recently, an unexplained tingling in the top of her spine, or shivers that raised all the hairs on her arms at the same time. It didn't pay to ignore feelings like that, she knew. They often portended something supernatural.

Hazel looked at her grandmother, who was lost in the next page of the book. "Does it say anything about how to get rid of them?"

"A large black cat, you reckon?" Her grannie shook her head. "Nope, a bit here about how to summon them but nothing about getting rid of them."

"Of course it doesn't." Hazel held the bed tight and swung her legs back and forth, like a child.

But her grannie held up one long finger, shushing her. "Wait a minute. There is a footnote though... It says here: Although they are a magical species, these creatures' behaviours are consistent with the cat species."

"What do you think that means?"

"It sounds like it means cats are cats," Grannie Em said. "Why? We don't have one of these here, do we?"

Hazel didn't see any harm in telling her what she'd noticed. "I'm thinking that we do."

"Oh, hell." Grannie Em put her hands on her hips and pursed her lips, staring at Hazel. "I did see something like that the other night, just after one in the morning. But I thought my eyes were playing tricks on me. See, you gotta trust your intuition," she said.

It looked like her mind was working flat out on what to do next. "I'll get to researching - there must be something more here..."

"Okay, thanks," she said. "If I can get five minutes peace from undead insects, I'm going to go and cook some lunch now. Tomato soup and toast, I think."

"Mm, save some for me." Grannie Em spoke the words absentmindedly, bent over with her long silver hair trailing down over the page. It was one of her favourite jokes. As a spirit, she didn't need to eat, but that didn't stop her getting hungry when someone else spoke about food. Hazel smiled to herself. Old habits die hard.

A high-pitched bark came from Bonnie downstairs.

Hazel started down the wooden ladder, hand over hand, thinking about her grannie. Was she really happy? She wondered what it would be like to have dry lips but never drink, to be starving hungry but never eat. To love but never feel the press of a loved one's lips or the warmth of a hug.

When she reached the bottom of the ladder, a voice said, "Hello, Hazel."

She turned around and found herself face to face with Mandy. "I'm sorry to be in your house like this. An eye for an eye, right?"

Vines lashed out from Mandy's wrists and bound Hazel to the ladder, cutting painfully into her upper arms and neck. In spite of the situation, she was impressed.

"Where did you learn how to do that?" Hazel tested the bindings but they didn't give at all.

"My coven back home." Mandy looked proud. "We are a lot more advanced, I have to say. But that's part of why I like it here—there's no pressure to be better than everyone else."

She heard a whine and saw Bonnie lying on the floor. *I'm okay, I've just aggravated my leg again.*

"If you scream, I'll do a little muffle spell," Mandy warned.

Hazel nodded. For the first time, she realized she was really out of her depth with these witches, and she began to panic in earnest. The front door opened and Joel stumbled in.

"Don't—" she started to say, but he was slammed into the ladder and bound with the same vines as her. The plant pots on the bookcase crashed to the ground, and a photo on the wall slid down at a crazy angle.

Joel railed uselessly against the limits of his movements, red-faced as a cartoon bull snorting air through its nostrils.

"What are you doing here?" she hissed across at him.

"I don't want to be here, trust me," he grumbled. "Rather stay far away from all this weird shit."

Hazel talked out of the side of her mouth. "So what happened?"

"I came outside because I heard a really loud buzzing sound. Like thunder, but it was fine outside," Joel said. "And Kirsten was out there. She told me to come and find you." His whisper sounded very cross.

"Uh, yeah, she can be very persuasive," Mandy put in, from the other side of the room. Hazel remembered the way

Kirsten's voice had reverberated around inside her mind, commanding. "Quiet, now."

Hazel wasn't about to be silenced. "Why do you listen to her, Mandy?" she asked, keeping her voice calm and even. "You're a successful woman, with a great job. I think you're actually a nice person too," Hazel said. "Just do what you want to do."

Mandy paced towards them and turned on her heel. "You think I'm a nice person? What do you have to base that on? I definitely wouldn't be where I am today, if it wasn't for her. I'd do anything for Kirsten. She gave me Con—"

"Confidence, I know." Hazel said, glumly.

Joel had started kicking the ladder, which was jolting Hazel, rattling her teeth.

"Stop," she hissed. She didn't want to do anything to provoke Mandy.

"Yes, stop that," Mandy said, straightening her orange top. She calmly reached out and sent a purple magic into the vines.

Joel grunted, and Hazel turned her head to see thin violet lines unrolling down the veins in his arms where the plants touched them. His head dropped to the side.

"Joel? Are you okay?" She turned to Mandy, fists bunched at her sides, shaking with anger. "What have you done to him?" Her voice sounded unbearably loud to her own ears.

Mandy wrestled with herself. "Just a simple spell to make him... sleep. You'll easily find an antidote."

"Well, reverse it! You don't want to be a monster. So don't be one, Mandy."

"Once you start, it's hard to stop," the other woman said. "You always have to be the one that shows no mercy first because the other person definitely won't."

"You don't know me," she went on, looking down at Joel, whose neck was exposed in a terribly vulnerable way as he slept. "I had my daughter and then I was unemployed for years. Just because I had to look after my child as a solo mum. There was so much competition for jobs back home. Do you know how hard that is? I couldn't buy her proper shoes for school. I became depressed and couldn't look after her, and they were going to take her off me."

Hazel blinked a few times, as salty tears pricked her eyes. She could feel the emotions coming off Mandy in waves, conflicted and complex.

"They were going to take her away. You've seen her, you know that she's the most—"

Mandy's voice cracked, and she took a few deep breaths. She was standing in the light of the kitchen window, and half her top glowed a bright orange. Hazel looked thought again of the light and shadow of magic, how one didn't exist without the other. Witches were all straddling the line each day. Making choices to protect those they loved.

"Kirsten and my brother were visiting and saw how bad it was. She offered me confidence in exchange for a year in New Zealand helping her out. I was desperate. I didn't know that helping her would mean meddling in people's lives."

Yes, but how, Hazel thought. *How do you give someone confidence?*

CHAPTER SIXTEEN

Hazel racked her brains to think of some magic she could do to get free. She was simply too out of practise to know all of those basic, useful spells. Joel was leaning over and pulling the vines uncomfortably tight around her chest.

Bonnie struggled a bit trying to get up and looked over at her. *Someone's outside.*

She heard a car door slamming out the front. It sounded like her mum talking loudly to her dad out the front. But that didn't make any sense at all.

After what felt like a long time, a light knock came on the front door. "Hazel," came her dad's voice.

The door opened and her mum walked in, blonde wavy hair puffed out around her face. "Oh, what's going on?"

"Aster? What is it?" said her dad, catching up.

They both seemed very calm for two people walking in on their daughter bound to a ladder. They couldn't yet see Joel or Mandy. Hazel's relief at seeing them soon turned to fear that they were walking into a trap. Her mouth went dry.

"Must be great to have Mummy and Daddy to call on."

Mandy said quietly, not looking at Hazel. She was focused on the spot where her parents would appear from the hallway in just a moment.

"I didn't." She was a little confused about why they were there. Hazel widened her eyes to show them not to come forward. But they kept on walking.

The vines crept from Mandy's hands and lashed themselves around her parents and they were slammed together in the hallway, vines covering their bodies from neck to ankles.

"Shitting shit!" Harold yelled. Aster just squeaked, as if all the air was squeezed out of her.

Mandy put her hands on her hips, looking from Hazel to her parents and back. "Oh, where is she? Does a witch have to do everything herself?" She worried at her bottom lip for a minute, straightening her blouse. Then she marched out the door, presumably to get Kirsten.

"Mum, why did you let… what are you guys even doing here?"

Aster looked at her, and a calm smile spread across her face. "It's alright, Hazel."

"Come on, love, I'm just about due for a cuppa tea," Harold said. "This isn't exactly comfortable, you know."

Hazel couldn't believe her dad said that, but Aster whispered something, low and insistent. A rustling came, and the vines slowly gave, just a little, until they had loosened enough for Aster to move her hands. They dropped to the ground and lay there, unmoving, just a pile of innocent leaves.

"I just asked nicely," her mother said, brushing the bits of leaves from her clothes. "You do have to be patient with plants. They work on a different cadence from us."

She whispered at the plants still covering her dad, which loosened. Soon he was rolling his shoulders around, and kicking his foot out, emitting light groans as his joints clicked.

"Ooh, I must be getting older," he said, with a wink at Hazel. "Clever lady, isn't she?"

Aster came over and whispered what sounded like Latin, gently touching the leaves on the vines that bound Hazel's wrists.

"Is this the boyfriend?" Aster hissed, getting rid of the vines gradually, so Joel tumbled ever so slowly to the floor. Hazel caught his head and cradled it on her knees.

"Kind of," Hazel squirmed uncomfortably. She wasn't ready for the part of her life with Joel in and the part of her life with her family of witches to meet yet. She wasn't confident enough of her own role in either.

"You've put him in danger, though." Her dad pointed to Joel.

"What has happened to him?" Aster asked, and Hazel laid his head down gently. "He looks like he's had a low dose poison. I'll make a salve up— "

Hazel looked at him, where he lay slumped on the ground, on top of the scattered vines. Dark blue lines marched up the sides of his neck. *Oh Goddess*, she had done this.

"Guys, what are you really doing here?" Hazel asked. She knew she sounded grumpy. "I'm an adult," she said, flopping onto the couch, just to complete the teenage stereotype.

"Don't get all worked up," her dad said.

"We've had the same thing before," her mother said. "Just after the last Secret Keeper was initiated."

"I think it was on Beltane, you know Halloween, I think about 1991?" Here he looked at Aster, and she nodded.

"It was my sister," she put in. "Briar went and did some stupid things. Must be some sort of rebellion of the soul after being bound to the new vows. Briar knew that we had to keep an eye on how you were going. She sensed that you were in danger last night. About nine pm, we got a call and she told us to come and stay with you for a few days."

Auntie Briar, Hazel thought. She should have known that Briar would know what she was feeling before she knew it herself. She always had.

Her dad put his hands in his pockets. "Is it about time for a cuppa yet?"

Aster flapped her hand at her husband. "Not yet," she said. "Still, we didn't expect to find you in this sort of situation. It's very serious. You've got to let the coven help you, Hazel. You're a part of something bigger than yourself."

"Why didn't she send Fritha over to check on me? Or ring up herself?"

"The tarot cards told her you needed the whole coven. And you do," said Aster. "They will be here in a minute. I'm happy we arrived when we did."

"And why the heck didn't she just tell me all this beforehand? This morning I fought off a pack of undead bees." Hazel laughed, but it felt like she wanted to cry.

"Hazel, there really are some things that you have to experience for yourself. If anybody had told me what it was like to have children before I had them, I wouldn't have believed it at all. What else have you been up to?"

"I snuck into Kirsten's house last night," she admitted. "I had to do something. I was so sick of feeling afraid every day, of not knowing what is coming or when. Of feeling like I have no control over anything." She looked at their shocked faces, then looked out the window. "Mum, Dad, we have to hurry. They will be back soon. I know what we have to do."

Hazel felt something clink into place, as when the whole coven was together. She looked out the window and saw Briar and Fritha standing out the front. They had started on protections for the cottage. But they were no use if the creature was sucking them away as fast as they made them.

She chewed on her thumb nail, considering. It was a cat. A huge magical cat, but a cat nonetheless.

"Hide, but be ready," she said to her parents. Hazel went and found some string, and grabbed a soft toy giraffe from a box in her cupboard.

She set the string out on the lawn, and held the other end, lying on her belly inside the kitchen. She pulled and twitched the string. Soon enough, the glowing eyes appeared in the branches.

Hazel waited.

Suddenly, it pounced. It was about the size of a medium dog and a dark brown. The giraffe never stood a chance.

Her dad stepped out of the door, magic sparking from his hands. Aster came from behind him, with another line of magic. The cat looked up at them, the giraffe hanging limply from its jaws, just as the three streams of energy hit it at once. At that moment, the injured look on its face at the unfairness of it, almost made Hazel laugh. It was just like any ordinary cat that has been tricked into a cat carrier.

Then the cat simply vanished. In its place was a pile of ash.

"Mum, can you look after Joel? I have to go and sort out some witches."

CHAPTER SEVENTEEN

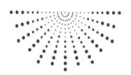

Hazel ran through the house out to the front, where Briar and Fritha had Mandy in some sort of protective circle.

"Where's Kirsten?"

"We haven't seen anyone else," Moira said. "This one was trying to leave. I think she realized she had met her match with us though."

"I did not," Mandy scoffed. "I was just getting tired, and maybe my reflexes were a little slow."

"Where would she have gone?" Hazel came up close to the circle to speak to her.

"I don't know." *She obviously didn't wait for me.*

"Mandy," Hazel said, softly. "I know you don't want to be here. Go back home... to your daughter."

"I can do anything here. I rented a house, got a job, hell, I even ran a half marathon the other week. To me, this is freedom. I got past your wards and summoned something powerful, using dark magic. That was me," she said, eyes flashing.

"You managed to do a summoning," Briar said faintly.

"It's alright. I dealt with it," Hazel answered. She didn't say I told you so.

She looked at Mandy, standing tall in front of her, and she saw fear flicker in her face. "You did those things all by yourself. You don't need anyone else. And now you should go back and give that wee girl a hug."

"I can't," she said, flatly.

"Because you promised *her* a year?"

"It's a deal signed in blood." *At the end of a year, I will have made enough money from the lizard potion that I can go build a wee cabin and live happily with Annie.*

Annie. The cherubic little face in the photo. How long had she already been without her mother? Two months?

"She needs you." Hazel said, and tears sprang up in Mandy's eyes. Her shoulders sagged a little. "And you need to find your own confidence, not be reliant on someone else. I know you understand. It's not too late to make the right choice. Burn the contract."

"Let her out, Auntie," Hazel said. She knew she had finally gotten through to Mandy. It would be fine to let her go. "Can you take her home?"

"Are you sure?"

"She's a good person. A good mother. She just got lost along the way." They accompanied her up to the road, with Mandy walking, dejected, between them. Hazel watched as Mandy got in the back seat and they drove away.

When Hazel walked into the lounge, it was completely transformed. The floorboards were clear of any greenery and sparkling clean. The pots that had been upset in the fracas were upright and the plants looked a healthy bright green.

Joel was lying on the couch, under a thick blanket. His face was pale and the purple veins seemed to have receded slightly. Her mother must have used a healing salve or poultice on him.

She peeped through into the bedroom, where Bonnie was sleeping on the bed, her face hanging off the side. She didn't open her eyes, and Hazel thought Aster must have made something to help her sleep.

A note on the table fluttered in the breeze. It was her mum's handwriting. 'It seems like everything is ok for now. Joel and Bonnie will be fine after some rest. We will get out of your hair until tonight.'

When she turned around, Joel's eyes were blinking open. "Where... What the hell happened?"

She went over to him, and put her hand on his forehead. "A lot happened! There were undead bees, and a huge magical cat. Oh, and a witch who has to set herself free."

"What... " He tried to lift his head, but plopped it back down on the cushion with a grunt. "Everything hurts."

"Yes, it will for a while. I'm so sorry." Her voice broke at the end of the last word.

"It's not your fault. That—"

"No, I think it is," she said, grabbing his hand. "I've been sticking my nose into Kirsten and Mandy's lives. In secret. But only because I was scared for you. I knew it was putting you in danger. My mum and dad and the rest of the coven turned up too, while you were..."

"Knocked out like a useless lump?" He lay his head back and shut his eyes for a second.

"Attacked, is what I was going to say. But I still can't believe my parents just arrived without letting me know first. I'm thirty-one years old. Do they think I'm that weak?"

Joel lifted his head again, and regarded her. "Weak? No way. You keep complaining that everyone is treating you like a child," he said, but he said it gently, tucking her hair behind her ear. "Maybe it's because you are giving them a reason to.

It's not weak to need other people sometimes. Everybody does. Maybe… you need to try trusting other people."

Hazel had the feeling they were no longer talking about her family.

"Yeah, I do," she agreed, softly. She stroked the back of his hand.

"I should get out of here before… "

Hazel's grannie slipped through the ceiling, squinting down at them.

"Did I miss all the fun?"

"Not now, Grannie," Hazel said. Joel fought to sit up.

"Don't struggle, dear. It will only make it worse," her grannie snapped. "Now, let's not be silly. Hazel told me you don't like coming here. That I give you the heebie jeebies? Your mother wouldn't have wanted you to avoid thinking about her or your dad. Dear Rosalie Anderton."

Hazel listened to the tiny creaks and groans of the house. She didn't know what Joel would do.

"Did you know my mum?" Joel asked. Two pale red patches appeared on his cheeks. He was frowning and his eyes looked suspiciously wet.

"I wouldn't say I know her, but I tried to send her a few messages, after your father died. She was really lonely when he was in the hospital. Then afterwards, she couldn't bear to fight to rebuild the house. I wanted to let her know that it was okay, that she was doing a great job raising you." She hovered closer to Joel. "I watched over you when you were a little lad, escaping from the babysitter."

"What?"

Grannie Em nodded. "Mr and Mrs Dowling couldn't keep up with you. You were always out under the trees, carving your name into them."

Joel's mouth gaped open. "I think your mum saw me one time, in the window. I like to think she knew."

CHAPTER EIGHTEEN

That night, Bonnie nestled into her leg in bed. When Hazel turned over for the twentieth time, Bonnie lifted her head.

Why aren't you sleeping? Are you worried?

"Not that they will come back. It's just… I'm not even sure. I'm thinking about that man I saw at the focus group."

Who is he?

"I don't know, but I knew his face."

Bonnie rested her head on Hazel's leg and she patted it automatically, scratching behind the soft ears. *From work?*

"No, I don't think so."

Is he a friend of Fritha's?

"Possibly."

Hazel thought of his face, trying to bring back the shape of his jaw and the way his hair sat. Suddenly she saw him on a black couch, leaning back and sighing loudly. She remembered his nose hair poking out from his nostril and the way his eyelashes were so light that you wouldn't think they were there at all from far away.

But she had been up close to him. She had been on the

same couch, and now the plush carpet beneath her feet came back to her. And the relaxing music. And last season's magazine, cool and smooth in her hands.

It wasn't him that was niggling at her subconscious. It was something that was behind him in the beauty salon.

"It's not him at all," she said to the dog. Behind him were the shelves full of colourful cosmetics; moisturisers, foundations, collagen supplements and a little purple bottle called Confidence 68.

Was this what Mandy had offered a year of her life for? A bottle of cosmetics? Was this the lizard potion that she had talked about?

Bonnie nudged her. *We haven't been for a walk in a long time. I can't wait for my leg to be better. It might help both of us when we can wander through the Green Belt.*

"Definitely," she said, looking at the silver face and puppy dog eyes. It had been too long since she did anything normal.

It's tiring for me listening to everything going through your mind.

Hazel reached down and stroked her head. Bonnie was right. She had been distracted for so long. No, she had been obsessed, if she was honest with herself.

It was a way to run away from those hard feelings; Joel and his moods, her responsibility to the coven.

She thought of Briar, who ran her business like a boss and was the perfect mother and partner to Moira. She seemed like she was always so confident. But she made mistakes and she let others make mistakes too. Perhaps that was what made an adult.

Maybe trusting herself was the first step. Tomorrow, she would meditate. And get back to swimming. She might even call Ellie and ask if she could get her aura cleansed.

CHAPTER NINETEEN

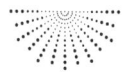

Hazel heard a knock at the door, and got up to open it. Joel was outside in a T-shirt and jeans. He flicked his sunglasses up on top of his head.

"Can I come inside?"

Hazel watched in amazement as he walked gingerly through the house, looking into all the rooms. When her grannie popped her head in, he only flinched a little.

How are you going now, young man?

"I feel better than I've felt in a long time," he said, taking an Afghan biscuit from the tin her mum had left. "I don't know why."

Hazel shrugged and smiled a secret smile. Her mother's medicines often had surprising effects on people.

She had to admit it had been nice having her parents to stay. She learned so much from them about living slowly. Life was measured in cups of tea, and magic was best when whispered to plants.

She showed Joel the pumpkin vines snaking over the ground and the new growth on the broccoli plant, watching him from the corner of her eyes.

"I'm sorry that I've been so distracted. I've got some... magical stuff going on." She decided to say it, wondering how he would react to the m-word this time.

"Yeah, I thought you must," he said. "It happens."

"I don't think you're a shit cook. Or a shit anything. I'd love to be like you. You're so calm. And you always go for what you want, without overthinking things. And I am really sorry for getting you caught up in it all, even though you don't want to be."

"That's just it. I kind of like getting caught up in it," he said. "It makes life interesting. I may be a bit grumpy sometimes. But you have to take the bad with the good, when you, ah, love someone."

Inside, Hazel was humming. Had he just said he loved her? Almost?

"If you're not busy on Sunday... do you want to come to my aunt's birthday?" Hazel asked, quietly.

"Sure," he said, pulling her close and kissing her soundly. He suddenly broke off, holding her at arm's length. "It's just normal right, nothing weird?"

"Yeah, it's at her café," she said, slightly out of breath. "There will be about twenty people there, like normal people. Nothing weird at all."

Moon Brew was sparkling with hundreds of hanging lights, that would have taken them hours to put up—if they were done by hand. All the tables had been pushed together, and jugs of Irish coffee stood between huge cakes and trays of food.

The living wall that took up all of the west side of the cafe was flourishing in flowers of red, yellow and purple, although it was autumn. Hazel gave it a sidelong look.

She had brought Bonnie with her to get her out of the house, and as long as she went slowly, her leg was getting better again. Her grey nose was visible through the doorway.

Joel bumped her with his elbow while he was loading a huge piece of red velvet cake into his mouth.

"Oy," she said, and bumped him back, so the icing went onto his cheek.

"Watch out," Fritha said, stepping back, as the two glasses of champagne in her hands spilled over the top. She set them down, and did a quick spell under her breath to clean up the mess. Then she sat down on the other side of Joel.

Hazel saw Briar behind the counter, so she chose the moment to talk to her alone. She was marking down what she needed to order in a little notebook.

"I've eaten so many of your Marmite pastries. Somehow, they ended up really nice."

"They were Moira's creation," Briar said, laughing. "I tried to talk her out of it."

"Are you having a good birthday?"

Briar looked up at Hazel, her gaze suddenly piercing. "I'm going alright so far," she said, carefully. "I can sense all the questions you've got."

"So you've still got your psychic abilities. I'm glad." As much as Hazel struggled with other people's thoughts, she couldn't imagine who she would be without them. She loved helping people, and people hardly ever knew what they really wanted. Mind reading was as much a part of her as her red hair, or her pointy chin.

"It's been almost like a grieving process for me," Briar said. "Like saying goodbye. Moira's been great, taking on extra shifts and looking after the laundry at home."

"Oh. That sounds awful," Hazel said. "Sorry I haven't been around."

"I know it's been a really hard few weeks for you. I did it that way on purpose, so you came into it with an open mind. Have you had anything weird happen since the initiation, Hazel?"

Hazel waved a hand around to indicate her life. "I mean, I'd be surprised if a day in my life wasn't weird at this point."

"Anything unexplainable," Briar pressed. "Like something that felt surreal, a memory, a person's voice?"

"Well, I did have a strange sense of déjà vu one day," she said, slowly. "In the Exchange. I was just walking through and felt like I'd been there before, in that exact spot, except the memory was *loud*, with the shadows falling over me and the whispering of the trees."

Briar rapped her hand on the counter. "Good," she said. "It's working."

"Does that mean something?" she asked. It seemed as if her aunt was willing to talk about it now.

"Oh, yes. It will start happening more and more. It might have seemed like nothing changed after the ceremony, did it? But the information is in there somewhere. We just have to unlock it."

"Are you going to help me, then?"

"Yeah, if I ever get five minutes away from this place," she said. "How do people drink so much coffee?"

"You love it," Hazel said. And her aunt smiled, and put her arm around Moira who had come over to see what they were talking about.

"Unfortunately, yes. It doesn't always love me though." The plants on the living wall seemed to lift up, as if hearing the affection in her voice.

Hazel just sat down with the others and her phone vibrated in her pocket. "Just give me a minute," she said. "Work email."

The email was sent to her work address, but the sender's name was Amanda Kennett. Hazel scanned the screen in amazement.

'To Hazel,

I found your email address through your work. I didn't think you'd mind me snooping a little as you know so much about me.

As this reaches you, I'll be winging my way back to England. For that, I can't express how grateful I am to you for setting me free. I can't wait to see my little girl again and hug her so tight.

I waited until midnight and burned the contract in the gas cooker. Immediately it felt like a weight had been lifted. I could see the past few months clearly. It was like a huge pyramid scheme! But you saw that, didn't you?

I tried to tell my brother but, sadly, I think he is too much a part of it. In the end, I didn't let him know I was leaving in case he tried to stop me.

Not everything you did was good or fair. But just know that I consider you a worthy foe, if not a friend.

Please just do one more thing for me. Stop her from doing the same thing to other people.

Best,

Mandy'

She let out a low whistle. Joel and Fritha looked over at her.

"Mandy has gone back to England. I'm so happy for her." Hazel sipped some of the champagne, feeling the bubbles pop and fizz on her tongue.

"So you were right?" Fritha asked. "She didn't want to be here."

"No, she didn't. She lost her way there for a while. And everyone needs to be given a second chance. But she's a really intelligent woman—competitive, intuitive, and determined. I have a lot of respect for her."

"Stubborn. Ruthless. Scary. I, for one, am glad she's gone," Joel said, lifting his arm up to draw Hazel in. He smelt of wood shavings and whisky. He was drinking Irish coffee now, and lifted his cup up. "I'd like things to remain completely normal for a while."

Hazel smiled and nestled in next to him.

Normal. She couldn't think of anything better.

The End

A NOTE FROM K M JACKWAYS

Hello! I hope you enjoyed Boundless Magic. Hazel and Joel will appear in another book, Blaze of Magic, coming soon. Please sign up to the newsletter to find out about new releases.

If you liked Boundless Magic, please consider reviewing it on Amazon or Goodreads. Every review helps!

Want more witchy fiction? If you'd like to find out more about us and our books, check out our website at www.witchyfiction.com

ABOUT THE AUTHOR

K M Jackways is a freelance writer and mother of two based in Canterbury. She loves shady green places and teaching animals to talk. Her fiction has been published in various magazines and anthologies, including The Best Small Fictions 2019. She has lived in random places, from Dunedin, New Zealand, to Bordeaux in France. Her stories expose the hidden lives of the past and the future, inspired by her background in psychology and linguistics.

EXCERPT FROM A GAP IN THE VEIL
BY SAM SCHENK

Gregory Able was going to save his first soul tonight.

He dropped his gym bag near a collection of broken gravestones in the shade of the state highway retaining wall, and fished a white candle and lighter out of the pocket of his denim jacket. An icy wind immediately tried to steal them from his grasp.

Greg swore, not for the first time, at Wellington's tendency to choose her moments. She wasn't going to have her way tonight. It was otherwise perfect — no people, the reach of tree branches just long enough to shut out the street lights and windows of parliament the next block over. The moon was bright enough to illuminate all but shadows beneath tree copses that hovered over faded grave markers.

After several sparks fell harmlessly from the lighter, he managed to get the candle lit. Shielding the new flame carefully, Greg approached a pair of benches contemplating a large rectangular plot marked by humble clay bricks. Swept clean, sanitised of moss and cleared of overgrowth, the vault exuded an air of quiet importance that trumped the unreadable grave markers inside. Had more care been taken in laying the dead, the other side would have been lulled to peace long before now, no intervention needed. But, here he was.

The crystals laid at star points around the edge of the graveyard were all in their proper places. Cloudy formations were already gathered around them, ready to work. His teacher would laugh at his refusal to call these clouds of energy "magic" like everyone else. Greg hadn't bothered to find a good name to call it either, but something about "magic" didn't seem right. He supposed it was a bit sparkly, a bit cold, definitely not produced from any gift he had. Magic was stuff cast from wands and words. This was something else. Something he was privileged to be able to connect with. He drew atmosphere from the clouds and twisted it around his fingers, eventually weaving the thread-thin result into a pentagon-shaped glyph. Once the shape was solid, each point connected with its brothers, he expanded each thread and pushed it into the air. A gesture brought it down around him, where it seared into the ground as cleanly as a laser burn. The wind quieted. The twisting flame stabilized into a thin, smoking line of heat. Colours and textures swirled out from around it, eventually clasping the remaining cloudy material into doorways to the veil.

Greg felt his body begin to relax. This was his place.

He knelt in the narrow space between the benches, breathing into focus the smells of soft moss and dirt tainted by the grease which somehow found its way onto his after-work clothes. He placed the candle on the ground at the exact centre of the five-point star.

Giving his shoulders a quick roll to release the last of the tension, Greg allowed his consciousness to wander. His attention spread between here and there. He reached out of his body to open a door.

He still looked like himself, but the weight of the physical world was gone. The veil cushioned his manifested projection like a warm bath in a sauna as he moved away from his body. He was surrounded by a humid atmosphere that would have clammed up his skin if he still had it. Cloudy, condensed energy swished between his spirit and body, throbbing along with his heartbeat. A pinch of tightness clasped at the base of his skull to remind him that he was still connected to the other world.

When Greg settled into his senses, he noticed a pair of familiar figures knelt over a ghostly chessboard. The first ghost already had a stern gaze prepared for him. He was a

moderately sized man in life, clean-shaven, broad in body, and dressed in plainly decorated vestments. His opponent was bearded and lean, with a tall hat and equally keen eyes. A watch with a gold chain peeked from his vest pocket.

"Evening, Robert, Lipman," Greg said, approaching.

"Good even', heathen." Robert sniffed. Lipman meanwhile, was deep in study of the board and raised his hand in greeting.

"Seen Elizabeth Hadley around?" Greg asked.

Lipman grunted for silence.

Robert grimaced at the other ghost but walked away from the chessboard. A living visitor made a much more interesting target for attack then his constant opponent, Greg supposed. The ghost's eyes pierced into his with zeal. "What would a worshipper of Lucifer want with Mrs Hadley? Think you I'll allow that sweet woman into the hands of the devil?"

Greg could feel his forced smile weaken at the edges. His stomach churned. Nevertheless, he pushed through, trying to keep his voice firm, but friendly. "Look, we can have this argument *again* later. Besides, she's hardly some colonial miss that can't fend for herself. After a hundred and fifty years she would know her way around. For now, I'd appreciate it if you'd let her know that I've found her body."

"What do you plan to do with it?"

Greg forced himself to hold eyes with the ghost. "I don't like your tone, old man. I'm just trying to help, and you know it. It's not as though I'm responsible for losing her body in the first place."

"What are you implying…"

"I'm implying that her body was lost. I'm telling you that I found it. Fact. I'm ready to tell her where it is so she can rest. Now, are you going to help me or not?" Robert held his eyes for a good twenty seconds longer than a modern-day politician. A ghostly hand thrust between them.

"Boys." Lipman interrupted.

"You stay out of this," Robert growled, turning to sneer at his opponent. "Mrs Hadley is not under your care."

"And you're the boatman for the goyim now?" The second ghost patted Robert's shoulder good-naturedly. "It's good business to clear this place of people who don't want to be here, that's all. You don't want her to get bored like the Wakefield kids, do you?" Robert shuddered. "A disgrace."

"A living who can turn book pages and use the internet is of much more use than us hanging around waiting for the first coming. We have a problem, Bobby, and you know it." Lipman walked back to the chessboard, moved a chess piece definitively into the centre of the board, and gave him a wide grin. "Mate in five."

Robert stared, wide-mouthed at the board, and moved back to the game. Greg let out a breath he didn't know he was holding. Lipman had saved Greg from a fire and brimstone sermon more than once, and he was grateful. "Cheers, Mr Levy."

Greg caught the hint of a smirk as Lipman turned away from them towards parliament where tiered seats were set into the hillside. Greg didn't notice them anymore. In the other world, he supposed they were charming, the largest piece of man-made architecture in the graveyard. In this world, they were mossy, covered over by the energy of the grasses and hillside. As a piece of art or construction, they were soulless and new — unlike even the highway retaining wall, which had at least been built with some sort of pride.

"Elizabeth, don't slink around in the schmutz. It's rude to keep a caller waiting," Lipman addressed the stairs.

A ghost's head emerged from the chipped marble veneer, tinted blue and green from her surroundings. Colonial attire followed, hanging on her corseted body as though it was being dragged by her head. Greg had seen her in the graveyard for months, stared at her even. But he had never been so close before. The clothing was tattered and dirty, her face drawn and tired, her eyes a single dark colour. She looked like a fearsome ghost from some action thriller, compared with the orderly appearance of Robert and Lipman.

He held out his hands so she could see them, the aura from his spirit self growing brightly to contrast with her near invisibility. Greg couldn't stop his hands from trembling. "Elizabeth, my name is Greg."

She manoeuvered behind Robert but didn't say a word. Maybe she couldn't. The two ghosts abandoned the chessboard. The preacher placed his hand on hers. His eyes softened, as did his voice. "Maybe it is best that you listen to what this heathen has to say."

"It's not out of character to trust a heathen when you have bupkis yourself." Lipman snickered.

"Be kind." It was Robert's turn to ignore Lipman. His nasal British accent was particularly prominent when he felt he had the higher ground. He floated away from Elizabeth towards Greg. "Remember you are in the presence of the fairer sex."

Greg gritted his teeth against a rebuke. He couldn't imagine there had been much time for coddling when Elizabeth was alive. Unwilling to draw this out any further, Greg steadied himself before addressing her again. He hoped his face was genuine.

"Elizabeth, those who want to move on should do so, and I'm here to help. Many of the spirits that linger here do so because their body can't be found." When he gestured to the vault, the sight of his body: still, breathing deeply in a meditative pose, drew his spirit form towards it. He resisted — straining against the compulsion, forcing himself to ground to the earth, adding weight to his spirit self to avoid moving forward. "I've managed to track the path your body took after you died. It's in the vault, Elizabeth. If you'll come with me, I'll guide you to it. Then you can decide whether you would like to stay or go."

Elizabeth drew nearer to Robert, who fixed Greg with a protective stare. But when the old preacher spoke again, his voice had lost its edge. "It's your choice, my dear. I believe you should go before you lose any more of yourself. Loath as I am to trust your soul to this… necromancer, it is too precious to lose to madness."

"If I were a necromancer, I'd wave my hands and you would all be gone, " Greg growled. "Show a little gratitude for the number of hours I've spent figuring out how to make this work."

Elizabeth gazed at the side of Robert's head, then cautiously back at Greg. Finally, she floated toward him.

Greg brightened. "Great, come this way… please." The last was added after a sniff from Robert.

He moved into the vault, deepening his connection with the earth with each step. He chose another anchor point — far below the surface, well below the vault, and increased his connection to it. The farther away from his body he moved, the more the connection at the back of his brain began to tense, itching as the cord twisted against his skin. He was drawn to touch it, to turn and see the source of the pressure on the back of his head. What he saw instead was Elizabeth, following at the edge of vision, her transparent hands folded against her tattered skirts.

By the time they had passed from sediment into hollow, stale air, the clawing at the back of Greg's head had tightened against his brain. He wasn't that far away from his body, nowhere near enough to worry, but moving through the vault was like travelling kilometres while listening to radio static. The interference made sense. The vault was home to some thirty-seven hundred named bodies, plus a few extras, not that he'd counted.

The interred bodies were mostly placed in long lines, veils respectfully laid over each. Some had deteriorated so much that you had to look hard to recognise any humanity at all. But he knew enough to sense when something didn't belong — in the walls, below the benches, in pieces here and there, some far beyond the vault marker above. The veil marked them with the guilt of the handler.

Elizabeth faltered behind him.

Greg couldn't afford for her to stop, but when he tried to turn, the connection stiffened and pulled against his head, threatening to drag him backwards. "Elizabeth, you have to keep moving. Come forward. It's not much farther."

The ghost let out a soft moan, but he sensed her move towards him. Before he could say anything else, a searing chill electrocuted through him. The next thing he saw was Elizabeth's head as it passed through his chest. Greg's thoughts flooded and merged with Elizabeth's.

He couldn't move. He was drenched in her misery. The weight of her insecurities tumbled over him, each thought driving pieces of humanity away.

She had never thought much about the afterlife. She missed her husband who had. She was so far away from family and everything she knew, and now she was stuck here, without him. He was her only connection. The land, the faces, the activities, everything was foreign. The corpses lying in the vault were reaching towards her with a thousand sharpened javelins, ready to spear her over and over again onto eternity. There were no friendly spirits to comfort her besides this living descendent of people she didn't know. Was being mad worse than spending eternity here? Where was her husband? Why had he moved on without her? Why was she still here?

Why wasn't Maddie here?

He wanted nothing more than his wife's arms around him. It was difficult to breathe, even though he knew he wasn't breathing. He felt the connection to his body throb with his increasing heartbeat. He felt like it would break his consciousness apart.

The glimmer of hope at the edge of their shared thoughts tore him away from his selfishness: maybe this could all finally be over for her. Greg glanced at Elizabeth, her ghostly form shivering as the veil's clouds flickered through her. She was in pain, the memories cycling over and over through her mind. She couldn't see past them. Any pleasure that she'd had in the afterlife, looking after her children and their descendants, influencing their lives in any small way, had faded into the background.

He focused, drawing on the small cloud of gathered energy hovering against the body like a beacon. He remembered how excited, how sure of himself he'd been as he marked it. The feeling, the pattern of the energy around it was the same as Elizabeth's. These broken cords were similar to his own connection to the physical world, the frayed ends swarming with energy. He'd stared at them for weeks. Physical channels had offered the key to her name: libraries, history books, genealogies. He'd meditated, stalking the feeling of her until he was absolutely sure.

Greg needed to channel those feelings, get the job done. So

much work, and finally, here she was, trusting him with her last shred of humanity. After shifting past several dozen half-rotted remains, down several levels, he found it. Greg struggled to lift his arm well enough to urge Elizabeth to move in front of him.

"Here you are, or…were."

Elizabeth moved from his side, eyes locked to the corpse. As she drifted nearer to it, energy collected from the thick atmosphere, and one of the thousands of connections dangling in the vault reconnected again. Her transparent figure started to fill out, but it didn't stop there. Soon, she was glowing with golden light. An otherworldly breeze brushed her clothes clean. The pressure around Greg's projection loosened, just a little bit.

When Elizabeth turned back to him, her face had substance, as though she had breathed moments ago. Her eyes — human and elegant, judged the miserable, crumpled shadow that he had become. Without a word, she leaned down against her remains and disappeared. No fanfare or fuss, not even a thank you. A ghost was gone from the world and onto the next, wherever that was.

Greg hovered, shaking, as the shared sensations rolled across his mind and spirit. He waited to feel like himself again. Though Elizabeth's doubts were sucked away from him like a vacuum, his own remained.

Disappointed, feeling dirty and exhausted, his head buzzing from the static of the vault, Greg turned back towards the surface. He should feel happier. This was the first step in clearing out the congestion in the vault. Instead of being able to luxuriate in a success he had worked for months to achieve, he couldn't get Maddie's face out of his head. He needed a drink, followed by a shower.

Lipman was waiting on the bottom row of seats when Greg regained control of his gravity. He waved Greg over past the chessboard, pieces now littering the floor. "The air is a bit cleaner. Mazel tov."

Greg wasn't sure if that was a question, but he sat next to the ghost anyway. "All done."

Lipman placed a hand near Greg's shoulder but avoided touching him. "You're a mentsh, lad."

"Thanks, I think."

Greg caught a glimpse of Robert out of the corner of his eye. Arms folded, he observed the scene from the top of the highway retaining wall. When he realised he'd been noticed, the preacher turned and floated over the highway toward the upper graveyard.

"Don't mind him," Lipman advised. "That meshugenah preacher thinks gentile souls are his responsibility rather than God's. You can't change a lifetime of beliefs, even after another couple of lifetimes."

"I'm going. It's another hour up the hill for me." Greg's voice sounded tired even to him. He wanted to avoid a round of debate with the philosopher if he could help it. The chess pieces began to assemble themselves into their right order again under Lipman's stare. "You should go into town, celebrate with a pint for all of us who can't. Have one for Elizabeth. Meet some person to help you warm up for the night." "I am still married, you know."

"You've given her plenty of time to come back. Face facts. She's out the door, son. There's no need to let yourself go to waste."

"Is it somewhere in the old testament that you can head out as soon as your partner does?" asked Greg.

"No, but it might well be in some version of the new one. No one need claim a piece of advice that makes sense for all. Besides, the people that remained are as diverse as the population. As many creeds as there are, there is a voice from each in my head. " Lipman turned to Greg as the chessboard reset to it's beginning state. "You helped a lost soul find peace, whatever comes next. You should celebrate victories, even ones more insignificant than this."

"Until next time, Lipman."

"L'chaim." The ghost threw his hand up.

Greg dove back into his body.

Breath came to him suddenly. His heart heaved. Blood rushed through his veins. Sensation returned to his eyes, brain, fingers and toes. It was cold, his body was soaked through from the windchill. Greg tested small movements first, followed by stretching his arms and legs. When he felt comfortable standing, he did a few squats. Finally, he stretched his arms above his head. His eyes hovered on the place where Lipman had been sitting. Greg wondered if he still watched, waiting for the graveyard to be left to the dead again.

Greg began a customary lap around the lower graveyard to clear his head. It took time to remember that he really was alive, after being surrounded by the veil's atmosphere for a while. Even in the physical world, cloudy expulsions from the veil sifted freely into the graveyard. When he was in his body, he had access to the same level of power. When Maddie left, he'd practically slept rough here.

The same chill slithered through him again. A surge of loneliness clenched at his gut, as raw as that first night alone. His pride and a locked cupboard had kept his fingers away from the phone. The edges of his eyes felt tight and heavy, ready to let loose with tears that he wished he could blame the wind for.

It passed as quickly as it had come on, leaving him staring into a cracked stone in front of him. What was going on?

Greg altered course to the upper graveyard, trying to shake it off. As he stepped onto the pedestrian access which crossed the highway, cars hurtled through the wind below. He measured the distance across the crevice for a moment, comparing the bottom of the upper graveyard and the top of the lower with his eyes — trying to imagine the shape the graveyard had once taken. There had been outrage at the suggestion to disrupt the graveyard in favour of the highway, but in the end, the powers that be had won out, as they usually did. Progress swept away much of history, but usually, it had enough respect to leave the dead in peace.

Even in the upper graveyard, where graves were organised into rows or sections, most of the markers were only remembrances now. Away from the main walkways, some were too close together, others at odd angles. The mind did circles when it tried to rationalise the shape of a body underneath. Earthquakes were responsible for some of the shifting, but others had clearly been moved, their contents now situated in the vault.

Not everyone had been dragged back from the world beyond, but the older ghosts were more active than the modern ones. Some were dressed in stiff colonial attire, or homemade suits and shifts, going about their business as though they were still alive, pretending that this was their world, like Lipman and Robert. Others were degrading, like Elizabeth.

Even thinking about her caused Greg to shudder. Miserable, lonely, dirty, and cold, he wrapped his hands around his upper arms against the chill that flowed into his body from the wind and outward from his spirit. He hadn't thought of Maddie in months… not really, anyway. And now, her memory hovered over him like an open wound. He had only saved one soul since she left. It seemed like an eternity ago.

Greg worked his way back down to his gym bag in the lower graveyard, packed up, and found his way onto Bolton Street. Facing uphill towards home, Lipman's advice didn't seem too bad after all. Something about the long walk didn't feel appealing yet.

The Terrace, just downhill, was deserted of its corporate patrons at this hour on a Wednesday. He found himself down a pedestrian access wandering towards the CBD, where the streets were just as deserted, but the occasional speaker could be heard from late-night joints upstairs. Finding the route to none of them without having to travel up and down alleys, Greg decided to give it up and cab home. Then, he noticed a pair of welcoming doors were opened to reveal a staircase upwards, with bright chalk signage inviting patrons in.

Want to read more? Click here to get A Gap in the Veil by Sam Schenk now!

MORE WITCHY FICTION BOOKS

Need more witchy goodness in your life? Check out the full list of Witchy Fiction books below!

Succulents and Spells (Windflower One), by Andi C. Buchanan: Laurel Windflower is a witch from a family of magic workers - but her own life is going nowhere until Marigold Nightfield knocks on her door. Marigold is a scientist from a family of witches, and she's in search of monsters. What lies ahead could reveal all Laurel's shortcomings to the woman she's trying to impress… or uncover the true nature of her power.

Hexes & Vexes, by Nova Blake: Small towns are full of gossip, and Mia is pretty sure that no one in her hometown of Okato has ever stopped talking about her. Cast off by her best friend, blamed for a local tragedy – Mia had no choice but to run away.

Now, ten years later, she's being dragged back.

Witching with Dolphins, by Janna Ruth: Friends before magic (or boys) has always been Harper's prerogative. Her best friend Valerie is everything she is not: beautiful, confident, and the most powerful witch on Banks Peninsula. They might not see eye to eye on everything, yet, when a sinister scientist threatens their coven, Harper is willing to give up everything: the man they both love, her life, or even the little magic she has.

Holloway Witches, by Isa Pearl Ritchie: Ursula escapes to Holloway Road leaving her former life in tatters following a bad break-up. She's looking forward to a quiet respite in a cozy cottage with a lush garden and lots of bookshelves, but instead she can't shake the eerie feeling she's being followed…

Familiars and Foes, by Helen Vivienne Fletcher: Adeline yearns for family, but for years, the closest she's gotten is her assistance dog, Coco. When a frightening encounter with a ghost brings an old friend back into her life, it seems like Adeline's about to find the companionship she's been missing. But her crush might have to wait. As the ghost's smoky presence increases, Adeline feels its hold on those around her tightening dangerously.

Overdues and Occultism, by Jamie Sands: That Basil is a librarian comes as no surprise to his Mt Eden community. That he's a witch? Yeah. That might raise more than a few eyebrows. When Sebastian, a paranormal investigator filming a web series starts snooping around Basil's library, he stirs up more than just Basil's heart.

Riverwitch, by Rem Wigmore: Self-taught witch Ashley Robinson spends most of her time on community work and picking up litter. When something goes badly wrong with the Waikato River, Ash is determined to get to the bottom of it. If only Bryony Manu, the other witch in town, could put aside their arrogance to help.

Jingle Spells: A mysterious child is spotted swimming far from the beach. A woman searches for a ghost in a blacked out hospital. One witch introduces her lover to her family, while another takes care of a magicaholic baby dolphin in her boyfriend's absence. A young man bonds with his pet eel, and yarnbombers accidentally summon something otherworldly. Jingle Spells is a collection of fun, quirky, and witchily magical Christmas stories by seven Witchy Fiction authors.

Microscopes and Magic (Windflower Two), by Andi C. Buchanan: Marigold Nightfield's life changed when she absorbed the magic stored in a family heirloom. Now, she's part of a growing network of magic-working scientists who are trying to change the world for the better, and has a girlfriend from a sprawling, powerful, witchy family. But when her girlfriend's work is destroyed by possible sabotage, and strange things start appearing in Wellington's green belt, Marigold's amazing new life starts to unravel. She'll have to not only draw on her scientific background and magical abilities, but make new connections and grow in confidence to face this new threat.

A Gap in the Veil, by Sam Schenk: As a mechanic, Greg can fix just about anything—except his broken heart. When a visiting musician dials up the charm after a gig in town, Greg's life looks to be taking a turn for the better. His plans to keep things simple between them are complicated by the awakening of a spirit bent on corruption. Greg must make choices between appearing distant or bringing his new friend into the fight, all the while saving Wellington from a past it had almost forgotten.

Raven's Haven for Women of Magic, by Anna Kirtlan: Cassandra Frost has zero interest in fortune-telling or brewing foul-smelling things in cauldrons, and much prefers the company of non-magical folk. She does her best to keep her powers under wraps to protect the secrecy of the Wellington witching community. But that's easier said than done when your grandmother lives in Raven's Haven for Women of Magic. Magical fireworks, mobility broom races and irresponsible use of cat litter spells are all part of the game for the witching retirement village residents. When Cassandra's forced to cast a spell in the open to save Adrian, a geeky graphic designer with secrets of his own, her two worlds spectacularly collide, and she learns the Haven is much more than meets the eye.